BANDIT'S TRAIL

Center Point
Large Print

Also by Will Cook and available from Center Point Large Print:

Blood Sky

This Large Print Book carries the Seal of Approval of N.A.V.H.

BANDIT'S TRAIL

Will Cook

CENTER POINT LARGE PRINT
THORNDIKE, MAINE

This Center Point Large Print edition is published
in the year 2017 by arrangement with
Golden West Literary Agency.

The text of this Large Print edition is unabridged.
In other aspects, this book may vary from
the original edition.
Printed in the United States of America
on permanent paper.
Set in 16-point Times New Roman type.

ISBN: 978-1-68324-558-2 (hardcover)
ISBN: 978-1-68324-562-9 (paperback)

Library of Congress Cataloging-in-Publication Data

Names: Cook, Will, author.
Title: Bandit's trail / Will Cook.
Description: Large print edition. | Thorndike, Maine : Center Point
Large Print, 2017.
Identifiers: LCCN 2017032735| ISBN 9781683245582 (hardcover :
alk. paper) | ISBN 9781683245629 (pbk. : alk. paper)
Subjects: LCSH: Large type books. | GSAFD: Western stories.
Classification: LCC PS3553.O5547 B36 2017 | DDC 813/.54—dc23
LC record available at https://lccn.loc.gov/2017032735

BANDIT'S TRAIL

ONE

This was, Jim McClintock thought, the exact time of the year, the exact moment, when Texas was most beautiful; the rain had stopped but the scent of it still filled the air and the water lay in clear, mirror puddles along the station platform; and the rails, running off into the saddle between green hills seemed as though they had just been given a coat of silver paint. The May weather was warm and the sun was down low against the skyline filled with bold, bright colors and casting a light that seemed to make everything it touched brighter and larger than it had ever been before. The windows of the buildings uptown caught the sun and reflected it as bright orange with strong red tints and the clapboard siding lost its dullness and became tawny and bright, as though the wood had been freshly cut and not weathered for a score of years.

McClintock leaned his height against the wall of the depot; he had his legs crossed and his fingers idly checked the wrapping of a fresh cigar for any fracture in the leaf. He wore a dark suit and a vest with a watch fob and chain that his father had given him. His hat was pushed to the forehead, shielding the upper half of a hound-lean

7

face. Without glancing at the man standing next to him, he said, "With all the experience they've had, you'd think they'd be able to run a railroad on time." He dipped a hand under his coat for a match and briefly exposed a bone-handled revolver nestled in a shoulder holster. McClintock's face was thin and deeply lined; he appeared older, more grave than his thirty years warranted, as though he had spent his life under a hard discipline. He looked at Finley Burkhauser. "You give up talkin'?"

"There's no need to go thrashin' about like a short-tailed bull in fly time," Burkhauser said softly. He was in his fifties, tall like McClintock, and as hard as a railroad spike. From beneath his broad-brimmed hat he squinted at the distance, a spot where the train was to appear. "When it gets here we'll get on it and ride her all the way to Houston if we have to." His glance left the sweep of the country and turned to McClintock, pulling his eyes nearly shut so that heavy crow's-feet bracketed them. Burkhauser's face was like an old glove, scarred and weathered and his waterfall mustache was gray, with only a hint of the dark brown his hair had once been. "If there's a holdup on this train I give it to you straight-haired, the varmint will finish the trip stretched out in the baggage car." He puffed his lips and made a rumbling deep in his chest. "By God, a man's got his reputation to think of."

"Let me see that wire again," McClintock said.

"You've seen it."

"It ain't goin' to hurt to have me look at it, that's all."

Burkhauser hesitated, then swept his coat back and reached into a rear pocket. He wore a brace of long-barreled .44 Remington pistols and the small badge of the Texas Rangers was visible an instant before his coat fell straight.

McClintock unfolded the telegram and read it:

MAY 3, 1884

SERGEANT F. BURKHAUSER
LIBERTY, TEXAS

HOW DID YOU EVER GET A PROMOTION TO SERGEANT? I'LL BE ON THE HOUSTON AND TEXAS CENTRAL, WESTBOUND. PLEASE BRING YOUR SAVINGS. I WANT TO MAKE THIS VENTURE PROFITABLE. BRING A FRIEND TOO. YOU WON'T BE ABLE TO HANDLE THIS ALONE.

"No name," McClintock said.

"What did you expect him to do, send his picture?" Burkhauser took the telegram and refolded it, then put it in his coat pocket. "Probably sent a wire so it wouldn't be in his hand writing. I tell you this fella's smart."

"Smart enough to rob three trains in ninety

days and get away with it," McClintock observed.

"Not this time. He's just got too big for his britches."

"Wouldn't surprise me none if he didn't show, Finley. That is, it could be a trick just to get us on this train while he robs another one."

Burkhauser shook his head. "He'll be on the train. He's dared me. Made his brag. He'll back it up." A whistle called lonesomely in the distance and Burkhauser straightened slightly. "Pay a mind to the passengers that get on now. That wire was sent right here to Liberty, by someone who knew I was at the hotel. That's how I got it figured." His lips pulled into a stubborn line. "I'll get him this time or by golly I just don't see how I can face the captain again."

"He sure yells a lot, don't he?"

"Never mind that now. You keep an eye on the passengers as they come out of the depot."

The train was coming on beneath a roil of dark coal smoke and the passengers came out of the depot to stand on the cinder platform. There was a woman with a brood of noisy children and a weary, patient husband who wasn't much good in maintaining discipline. One of the children, a boy of six, wanted to run down the track and meet the train and started to, only he was halted a few yards on by a strongly built man in his young thirties. He shooed the boy back to his parents and tipped his hat and revealed a shock of wavy blond hair. The woman said something but McClintock couldn't hear it, then the man turned and went down the platform to stand. Several cattlemen stood in a clannish knot and beyond them, three farmers waited, suspiciously eying the cattlemen. Two drummers with their suitcases stood by the depot wall.

"He could be on the train," McClintock said.

"He could," Burkhauser admitted. "We'll see."

"You're goin' to feel awful foolish if he ain't, Finley. Be kind of hard to explain to the captain how you fell for a trick."

Burkhauser looked at him. "I'll tell you, Jim, you let me worry about any explainin', if it becomes necessary."

McClintock grinned. "I keep forgettin' you're a sergeant and I'm just a plain ol' corporal." The train was slowing now and it came into the station, brake blocks squeaking and chattering; it huffed on and clanked to a stop and the conductor got down with his step and polite manner. Engine and cars were leftovers from the war now twenty years past and both the engineer and fireman got down and hurried along, checking for hot boxes and anything else that may have fallen off, or was about to. The coaches were grimy and the once-bright paint was peeled and faded; Burkhauser and McClintock held back and were the last of the passengers to get on.

The sun was almost dipped now behind the hills;

11

the sky was a mottle of red and darker orange and the station agent lighted the lamps and the last rays of light on the window panes made them a brighter, richer yellow. The conductor waited until McClintock and Burkhauser got on, then picked up his step and waved the train in motion; it lurched forward and Burkhauser, in the vestibule, was caught off balance and hit his shoulder against the door frame.

He swore softly and entered the coach, moving to the rear of the train with McClintock right behind him. The coach was crowded and had the flavor of an old boot that hadn't been pulled off the foot for a week running. The seats were once a maroon, but time and wear had faded them and along the backs, soiled hands gripping them as an assist to leaving had soiled them black.

The train was in motion, lurching along, gaining speed; Burkhauser's destination was the gentlemen's smoking car just ahead of the caboose. He reached it and opened the door; the transition from the fresh air of the vestibule to the rank thickness of the smoking car was a shock that made him wrinkle his nose. Thirty years of packed cigar smoke had soaked into the wood, and around the spittoons, ten thousand misses had darkened the floor. There were chairs and tables for those who wanted to play cards; Burkhauser found a pair of chairs near the rear and nodded for McClintock to sit down.

Three men occupied the car; two read newspapers while the third played solitaire. The cattlemen soon came in with their laughter and noise; they sat down and immediately began to play cards and drink from a bottle one of them had in his coat pocket.

Both drummers came in with their sample cases; they were men with open, smiling manners, for friendliness was a part of their business. In time they made their way to the rear of the car and after they sat down, one took off his derby and wiped his bald head with a handkerchief. His glance took in Burkhauser and McClintock, then he said, "The weather's warm for May, ain't it?"

"Not too hot though," McClintock agreed.

"Yeah, just about right." The man offered his hand. "The name's Higgins. Albert Higgins. Hardware's my line."

"McClintock. He's Burkhauser. Army contractors. Livestock, supplies—you know."

"Well," Higgins said, "it's nice to meet men in the selling line. Everybody buys from a salesman but damned few understand him."

"How true that is," McClintock said. He nudged Burkhauser, who gave him a sour look. "Wouldn't you say that, Finley."

"If I was forced to."

Higgins looked at him seriously. "You have some bad luck, friend?"

"Put it that way if you like," Burkhauser

admitted. He took a cigar from his pocket and lit it and retreated behind the smoke.

"You ride this train much?" McClintock asked.

Higgins held up a finger. "Every month. Hate it. The line's a wreck. Coaches are dirty and equipment's shot. But it goes to Houston and my main office is there." He sighed. "And now we've got these rash of holdups. I was on the train the time it was held up, you know."

"Do tell," Burkhauser said, his manner dry.

"Well, it's nothing to treat lightly," Higgins maintained. "Cleaned me out of nine hundred dollars in company money, that's what he did. Of course it was insured, but no man likes to have a gun stuck under his nose and told to fork over." He glanced apprehensively at Burkhauser. "Couldn't help notice when you reached for your cigar that you're packing some heavy artillery. It's my opinion that unless a man's pretty good he can get into—"

Jim McClintock smilingly interrupted him. "The fella who sold it to him told him where the trigger was and which way to point it." He glanced at Burkhauser and the frown on his face. "It gives Mr. Burkhauser comfort, and I say that a man his age is entitled to comfort."

"Boy, how you can talk," Burkhauser murmured and drew heavily on his cigar.

"He don't take to joshing, does he?" Higgins observed.

"Oh, it's just that he's been feelin' poorly lately. His boss has been after him somethin' fierce; it just seems that nothin' comes out right. Wouldn't you say that's the case, Burkhauser?"

Higgins looked from one to the other. "Say, you two are friends, ain't you?" He waited for his answer and got none and he got up and moved to another chair.

Burkhauser spoke softly. "You could talk yourself into some extra duty easy enough when we get back to battalion headquarters if you ain't careful."

"I've got extra duty now," McClintock said. He leaned back, an arm flung over the back of the chair. "Come on, Finley, admit it; you just couldn't get along without me." McClintock let his smile broaden. "Let me tell you how it was. You knew it wouldn't do to go it alone; the captain would scald you like a shoat for it. So you just looked around to see who was handy and thought of me, down there at Fort McIntosh, doin' nothin' but chasin' Mexican bandits and spendin' my evenings on some front porch, strummin' a guitar and singin' off key to a señorita. Yes, sir, Finley, you thought of me and said to yourself, 'Now here's the only fella in the whole Texas Rangers who'll work with me because I'm a stubborn, trouble-huntin' old fool who's sassed the governor and cussed the captain.' " He ticked off the points on his fingers. "One, we've worked together before and somehow I've learned to put up with you. Two, I knew you'd try and take this desperado alone if I didn't shag-tail and catch the first eastbound to Liberty and give you a hand. Three, I want to talk to you anyway because I've met a girl and I'm thinkin' about askin' her to marry me and you just spoiled my plans."

"What woman would have you? You ain't got good sense yet." He leaned forward a bit. "Jim, are you serious about some girl? Someone I never met and gave my approval on? Why, you ought to know better."

"I can pick my own woman," McClintock said. "You'd like her, Finley. I met her accidental like at Laredo; she was comin' down the stairs and I was goin' up and I took one look at her and just naturally smiled. Dogged if she didn't smile back."

"What's her name?"

"May." He sighed. "Later that evenin' I saw her in the dinin' room. Now you know I wouldn't walk up to a young woman's table just on a notion, but she looked at me and I looked at her and the next thing I knew I was sittin' there and we got to talkin' and it was after ten before we said good night."

"My, that sure is romantic," Burkhauser said dryly. "You meet a woman once and you're in love. Damned fool sprout!"

"I met her three or four times," McClintock said. "Her brother was some kind of a salesman and she'd meet him in Laredo; he went to Mexico a good deal. Sometimes he stayed down there for months." He sighed. "Finley, you'd like May. She's kind of a shy girl, but she's got a mind of her own. A couple times now I've started to bring up the subject of how I feel, but she's headed me off. Yet I get the notion that she didn't want to do that. You ever run into anything like that?"

"She didn't want to see you make a jackass of yourself, that's all."

"That's what I like about you, you're so damned understandin'. Point four, though, is how come you've passed me over for sergeant. I've got the time and you know it."

"Talk to me in another five or six years," Burkhauser said. He brushed his mustache as though hiding a smile behind his hand. "I knew I could count on you, Jim. You really ain't worth hell, but you're reliable. I've got to say that for you. Put it on your record too, if you insist."

"Favors from you I've learned to live without. You're the orneriest old goat I ever knew. The only reason I'm here is because I know your record: You somehow, through dumb luck I suppose, manage to bring in every man you ever went after. Through the years, by stumblin' along, you've built a reputation, but I'm here to tell you that this one may be more than you can handle."

"Why don't you just come out and admit that you like me?" Burkhauser invited. "Come on, it won't hurt you none." He chuckled and rolled his cigar from one corner of his mouth to the other. "Do you remember that time on the Rio Salado when we caught those Mexican bandits? My horse had been shot out from under me and we was outnumbered eight to one; I gave you an order to leave me and high tail it out of there, but you packed me all the way back to Laredo."

"You bled all over my good saddle," McClintock said. "Never did get the stain out. If you'd listened to me and hadn't went for a shoot out—"

"—sure, sure, but them bandits stayed south of the border, didn't they?" He smiled beneath the thicket of his mustache. "You was twenty then, Jim, and about as green as they come. But you stuck with me when it could just as well have got you killed. I always figured it was because you liked me."

"If I'd left you, how the hell do you think I'd have explained that to the captain?" McClintock said, keeping his face straight with an effort. "And speakin' of times, let's go back to Eagle Pass. Now just what the hell made you think you could outdraw the Rameras brothers anyway? If I hadn't been in the barbershop when the shootin' started—"

"Very timely," Burkhauser agreed. "I always said so. But I had the situation in hand. Well, I was on the ground, that's true—"

"Yea, a bullet in your thigh and another in your side," McClintock said dryly. "And the Rameras brothers still standin'."

Burkhauser pointed a finger. "Only because one fell against the hitchrack and it was holdin' him up. I drilled him dead center first shot. It's true that I was in a mite of trouble when you stepped into it, but I had 'em under arrest. They was just resistin' a little." He leaned back in his chair and regarded Jim McClintock. "I wanted you special on this job, because—well, I need a man I can trust with my life. We've been through a dustup or two. I didn't think you'd mind workin' with me."

"I'm here, ain't I?" McClintock let a smile build, then he chuckled. "Finley, the way I got it figured, someday you're goin' to bite off more'n you can chew and I don't want it on my conscience that I could have helped you and turned you down. But I'm goin' to have a hard time explainin' this to my girl, why I tromped across half of Texas just to answer your damned whistle."

"You know I got winnin' ways," Burkhauser said, smiling again. "It's just that we're both dancin' men, Jim, and we hear a new tune bein' played."

"Yeah, some music," McClintock admitted and stared out the grimy window at the passing landscape. The night shadows were darkening the land and he had no clear look at anything. Now and then he saw lamplight in the distance, a ranch or a railroad shack; the rest was night and hidden from him.

He and Burkhauser glanced up as the smoking car door opened; the father of the unmanageable brood of children they had seen on the station platform came in and wearily settled in a chair; he took a Moonshine Crook from his pocket and lit it, then sighed and looked around before speaking to no one in particular. "God, but it's peaceful in here." He puffed his cigar and folded his hands. "I'd buy a drink off any man that's got a bottle."

One of the drummers had one and offered it to the man, shaking his head when the man dug into his pocket and offered to pay. Three more passengers came into the car. The cattlemen continued to play cards; they had nearly a hundred dollars on the table and they talked softly as though determined not to disturb anyone. Without seeming to, both Burkhauser and McClintock studied the new arrivals; they were all in their middle thirties, wearing suits; they seemed intent on minding their own business and McClintock decided that they were strangers to each other, having only by accident entered the coach together.

The train was laboring up a long grade and the speed had dropped considerably but was now steady, as though the engine had taken on a second wind. One of the drummers looked at his watch and said, "Be in Morgan Tanks in another fifteen minutes." He put his watch away and smiled. "I ride this rattler so regular that I know every rail joint. We'll stop at the tanks for water and coal. It's the top of the grade."

The fretful husband said, "I suppose Emma will want to get off with the kids. It's like a woman. You take 'em somewhere and they got to go to the outhouse as soon as they get there. Any you fellas married?" He looked around and several men glanced at him, but no one said anything; it seemed to be something no one wanted to talk about. "Funny thing how a man can love a woman, need her, and at the same time find that she gets on his nerves." He looked around for sympathy. "You take kids—"

"You can have 'em," the drummer said dryly.

"Aw, I like kids," the man said. "I've got five."

"Maybe you don't know what causes 'em," the drummer suggested.

"Now that's real comical," the man said, his manner irritated. "You take a baby; they're cute as hell, but they bawl all the time and you can't hardly wait until they learn to talk like everyone else. Then they learn and jabber on and on and you wish to hell they'd shut up."

"You're just hard to satisfy," McClintock said. "I figure kids would be right enjoyable."

"You want a couple right now? Take your pick."

"I can get my own," McClintock told him.

One of the three men who had come in casually pulled a nickel-plated revolver from beneath his coat and said, "I hate to terminate this delightful conversation, but the time has come for you to give me your money." He was a slender man, not too tall, with sandy hair and clear blue eyes and a cool manner that held them motionless for an instant. The drummer swallowed hard, and nudged the other drummer who was dozing in his chair. The man came awake with a little snort, looked around to get his bearings, then moaned softly to himself and slowly raised his hands. The cattlemen stopped talking and playing cards; they let their hands rest on the table and watched the bandit.

Jim McClintock made no motion at all, but Finley Burkhauser reared out of his chair and reached for his portside pistol; he got his fingers around the butt and the bandit shot him high in the arm, spinning him around, sending him into the cattlemen's table, upsetting it and making them back quickly out of the way.

There was a moment there, a moment full of confusion and surprise and McClintock acted; he launched himself at the gunman, meaning to tackle him and he got his arms around the bandit's waist and then the bandit struck him heavily across the head with the barrel of the gun and McClintock fell, stunned and lacking the strength to get up.

One of the cattlemen lunged for the emergency cord and yanked it; the brakes went on with a screech and the passengers were thrown off balance. It was the right thing to do and the wrong thing, for Burkhauser, his face strained with effort, was sighting his other pistol and he triggered his shot as the train lurched, missing the bandit by three inches and breaking instead the glass in the vestibule door.

Without hesitation the bandit abandoned his plans and flung open the door and jumped from the train just as it was sliding to a halt. The conductor came in, angry, loudly demanding to know just-what-the-hell-is-going-on-in-here-anyway. He saw Burkhauser stagger to his feet, blood dripping down his arm and off his fingers. McClintock was moaning, getting to his hands and knees.

The train was stopped and one of the crewmen rushed in. He also wanted to know what the devil was going on, and everyone tried to tell him at once, except Burkhauser, who retrieved his lost pistol and clumsily holstered it. He went over to McClintock and helped him to his feet; the young man fingered the split on the back of his head.

"He jumped the train," Burkhauser said. "We may still have a chance." He started for the vestibule door but McClintock blocked him. "Get that arm fixed first. I'll have a look around."

McClintock stepped down from the train and a crewman came up with a lantern; he shined it in McClintock's face, then lowered it when he was satisfied with McClintock's identity. "Did you see a man jump off the train?" McClintock asked.

"Didn't see it. Heard someone ride off though."

McClintock got back on the train. Burkhauser had his coat off and one of the drummers was wrapping his arm tightly. "Well?" Burkhauser asked.

"He had someone waiting with a horse. One of the crewmen heard him ride off."

"Damn it!" Burkhauser said. "What I wouldn't give now for a horse."

"You're in no shape—"

"The hell I ain't!" He looked around as one of the cattlemen shouldered through. "What's your problem, friend?"

"I've got horses ahead in the cattle car," the man said. "Good blooded stock. No saddles though. You're welcome to—"

"We'll take two," Burkhauser said, getting up. "I'll give you a voucher from the State of Texas to—"

"Just see that I get 'em back when you're through," the man said. "The name's Shingles, Andrew Shingles. Got a place about ten miles south of Houston. Just ask for me. Everybody knows me around there."

Burkhauser nodded his thanks and turned to the conductor. "Do you have any rifles aboard?"

"Both the express guards have rifles."

"Fetch 'em then. And what ammunition you have. What are you waiting for? And get that cattle car opened up." McClintock put out his hand and Burkhauser slapped it aside. "Now don't start fussin' with me like a titty nurse, damn it. If that ring-tail thinks he can put a bullet in me and ride off without payin' for it, then he's got a lesson comin'."

"You'll fall off your horse in five miles," McClintock said.

Burkhauser stared at him. "If I do, I've got you to put me back on. You ready to go?"

"Why, you stubborn old goat, you don't think I'd let you go alone, do you?" He laughed and stepped down from the train and they went forward together, the crewman with the lantern walking ahead so they wouldn't stumble over the railroad ties.

The cattleman was helping the engineer and

25

fireman get two of his Arabians down; they were large horses with alert ears and fire in their eye. Jim McClintock whistled softly and the cattleman grinned. "I gave a thousand dollars for this pair. They can run down anything on the prairie." He handed the reins to Jim McClintock. "Not only do I object to having a gun pointed at me, but I'm carrying nearly twelve thousand dollars on me. The fact that he didn't get it makes me happy, but I'll be downright delighted if you catch him." He looked at Finley Burkhauser. "You sure he can ride?"

"He can ride," McClintock said and gave Burkhauser a boost aboard the near horse. The animal started to jump but Burkhauser gave him a lesson in discipline that didn't last long but was something to remember; he jabbed the horse with his spurs and sawed him around in a tight circle and drove him into the side of the cattle car. Then when the horse stood quietly, trembling, he said to McClintock, "You going to stand and gawk or ride?"

"Let's ride then," McClintock said and mounted up.

The conductor came up with some rolled blankets and a paper sack; he handed them to McClintock, saying, "I got these from the caboose. There's some sandwiches in the bag." He pointed in a southerly direction. "Likely he'll back track. Good luck. You want to send some kind of a message? When I get down the line to a telegraph—"

Finley Burkhauser turned his horse so that he faced the conductor. "You know what happened. Send the details to Captain George Fuller, Commanding Company D, Texas Frontier Battalion, Fort McIntosh."

"I'll take care of that, Ranger," the conductor said. He opened his mouth to speak again but Burkhauser had wheeled his horse and was starting off with Jim McClintock following him closely.

The train got underway again and they rode to the crest of a rise before looking back; the train was slowly inching up the grade to the tanks a few miles beyond; the lights of Morgan Tanks were visible, a pinpoint to the west.

McClintock said, "I guess it's occurred to you that he had someone waitin' for him with horses." He edged his horse around so he could see Burkhauser. The night was clear, warm for May, and the moon was not yet up. They were in hilly country with long ridges running north and south, and deep, broad valleys between them.

Burkhauser sat hunched over; pain was beginning to work on him and when he spoke there was only a tightness in his voice to betray it. "Before I ever got on that train," he said, "I spent two days studyin' maps of this country 'til I knew every draw and hogback for seventy miles. He won't run south; that would take him to the sea. My guess is that he'll cut west, cross the San Jacinto above the forks, then make a beeline for Fort Parker or Huntsville."

"That's damned near a hundred miles, a two day ride in this country, and then you'd have to push it." He shook his head. "My guess is that he'll head for Houston."

"He knows there's a Ranger detachment there," Burkhauser said. "No, was I him, I'd head 'cross country. He knows I'm packin' lead. He knows the conductor will wire ahead as soon as he reaches Morgan Tanks. Let's cut in a circle and see if we can pick up his tracks. The grass is fresh and tender; he'll leave sign a blind man could follow."

"All right, I'll cut a circle. If I find anything I'll signal." He started to turn his horse, then stopped. "You still bleedin'?"

"It's stopped," Burkhauser said.

"You got the bullet still in you?" He edged closer to Burkhauser. "The first chance we get—"

"Yeah, yeah, I know," the old man said. "You're wastin' time."

"Damned old hero," McClintock said and rode off, staying parallel to the tracks, and he studied the sea of thick grass until he found

28

what he wanted; a swath trampled by two riders. He could not see Burkhauser, so he stuck two fingers in his mouth and whistled shrilly, and a moment later did it again. Then he saw Burkhauser approaching.

The old man bent to study the ground. "Milling around here," he said, then pointed to a single trail circling back. "Smart. He crossed the tracks behind the train while we were gabbin'. You still think he ain't headin' north?"

"All right, so you made a smart guess," McClintock said. "But he ain't stupid either. Once he hits a road his trail peters out."

"I know what he looks like now," Burkhauser said. "His trail's never going to peter out until I've got him in jail." He kneed his horse around. "Let's go."

They moved across the tracks, picking up the trail there; it ran in a northwesterly direction and both could see that the rider was pushing his horse hard. For three hours they followed the broad sweep of a valley, crossed several creeks, then came to a rutted wagon road. The moon was up, shedding a bit of light, and there were some thin, high clouds and a bit of wind came up from the south, stirring the grass and making soft, whispering sounds in the trees that cluttered the valley in patches.

They rode for nearly a mile, then a dog started barking; they stopped and ahead they could see a dark mottle amid some cottonwoods and they could make out the outline of a barn and other outbuildings. A ranch house fronted the road and Burkhauser urged his horse on.

When they were a hundred yards out, a voice hailed them from some hidden place in the yard, a stern voice full of threat. "There's a rifle on you! Sing out or I'll shoot!"

"Sergeant Burkhauser! Texas Rangers!"

The man laughed and someone else laughed from a place near the barn. The man said, "I fell for that an hour ago! He stole a horse and made me fill a sack of grub for him!"

Finley Burkhauser swore softly. "The nervy bastard." He raised his voice. "We'll come in and make no move to our weapons. We have identification."

"Come ahead then, but you make a mistake and it'll be your last!"

"You've nothing to fear from us," Burkhauser said and rode forward.

They came on carefully and the man stepped out; he faced them with his rifle and they stopped. From behind them a boy of sixteen came up with a rifle and a lantern; he held the rifle in the crook of his arm while he lighted the lantern and when the man could see, he reached out with the muzzle of the rifle and lifted aside Burkhauser's coat, exposing the badge. Then he did the same to Jim McClintock.

"All right, get down. Come in the house." He turned his head and yelled. "Light the lamps, Jessie." He still covered them with his rifle and when Burkhauser slipped off his horse, he moaned slightly and drew the man's attention. "What's the matter with you?"

"He's got a bullet in his arm," McClintock said. "The same fella that stole your horse put it there when he tried to hold up the train."

"We'll take care of that," the man said. "Come on in." He stepped to the door and held it open for them. "Carl, you take care of the horses, and fetch some water when you're done with that."

Burkhauser stepped first into the kitchen; a gray-haired woman looked steadily at him and two young girls stood near a door, as though ready to flee. Burkhauser said, "Madam, I'm sorry to intrude."

"You sit right down here," she said. "Tass, help the Ranger off with his coat. And be careful of his arm." She looked at the other girl. "Fix a fire and make coffee, Addie. Don't just stand there."

McClintock put his rifle against the wall and moved around so the lamplight fell over his shoulder. The man said, "Name's Elmer Fry. My wife and daughters. It took us by surprise, sure enough. He came in, bold as brass, identified himself and we opened the door. Then he threw down on me with his pistol, helped himself and rode off."

"What was the matter with his horse?" McClintock asked.

"Went lame he said." Fry pulled a chair around and sat down facing Burkhauser. His wife handed him a small kitchen knife and he slit Burkhauser's shirt sleeve and examined the wound. Fry scratched his chin. "Looks small bore to me. .38-40 more'n likely. Well, we can get that out without much trouble. Jessie, you get what you'll need to bandage him up. Fetch those pain powders the doctor left here." He smiled. "Last fall Carl hurt his foot. The doctor gave him some stuff to kill the pain, but you know how boys are, tryin' to be tough all the time. He wouldn't take it. It'll come in handy now."

Burkhauser's expression was bleak and his complexion gray. He gave Fry a wan smile and leaned back in the chair as though immeasurably glad of the opportunity to rest. "You're a Christian, Mr. Fry, but I'd appreciate it if you wouldn't spend too much time with me. The fugitive has enough of a head start as it is."

"I guess he'll be caught soon enough," Fry said. "But you need to get that bullet out, Sergeant. You leave it in and you'll be fallin' off your horse before morning." His glance was raised to Jim McClintock. "It ain't only the young that's stubborn, is it?"

TWO

Elmer Fry was a man who liked to talk while he worked, and his constant prattle got on Jim McClintock's nerves, although he had to admit that it didn't slow Fry down any or cause him to bungle. He used a small button hook to probe for the bullet and he was better than some doctors who had to jab and wiggle around; Fry knew what he was doing and plopped the bullet into a shallow tin pan before Burkhauser could think to swear because it hurt.

The wound was cleaned thoroughly and bandaged and the arm put in a sling. The youngest girl served coffee and some sandwiches made with cheese and cold meat. Burkhauser leaned against the table, using his good arm to steady himself. Fry watched him for a moment, then said, "Them powders taking away any of the pain?"

"Yes," Burkhauser said. "It hardly hurts at all."

Fry folded over the torn end of the package and handed it to Burkhauser. "Instructions written right on it. You take it along." He leaned back in his chair. "You know, a man never really expects trouble around here. Got good neighbors and the Indians are all on reservation. So when this fella rode in and hailed the house, why I just lit the lamps and opened the door." He continued to study Finley Burkhauser with his eyes pulled close together and his eyebrows bunched.

Burkhauser said, "Something bothering you, Mr. Fry?"

"I guess you know who you're after."

"We both saw him on the train, yes."

"Funny he'd use your name," Fry said. "He said somethin' else just before he rode out. He said he'd see you in Fort Parker, if you didn't waste too much time gettin' there. I guess he was referrin' to your arm slowin' you down some."

"Is that all?"

Fry rubbed his chin. "No it ain't. He said he was goin' to Nacogdoches to catch another train."

"Well," Jim McClintock said, "you can't say he's bein' sneaky about it." He glanced at Burkhauser. "You figured out why he's baitin' you, Finley?"

"No. I never laid eyes on him before he stepped into the smokin' car." He slowly got up from the table. "Fort Parker's abandoned, fallin' down; he won't stop there long. Mr. Fry, would you have a couple of old saddles? I don't relish the thought of two days of riding bareback."

"I can spare a couple," Fry said. "It seems to me you might do better to head for Nacogdoches."

Burkhauser shook his head. "There's somethin' here I don't understand. He sent me a wire at Liberty, tellin' me he was going to hold up the train. Now he leaves this message with you. Wouldn't you follow him, Mr. Fry?"

"Yeah. If nothin' more than to find out what his game was."

"I know what his game is," Burkhauser said. "My purpose is to end it." He put on his hat and offered Elmer Fry his left hand. "Thank you for your hospitality. I'll see that your saddles are returned."

"You do it in your own good time," Fry said. "Carl, you go saddle the horses." He stepped to the door and opened it.

Burkhauser turned to Fry's wife and daughters; he bowed slightly, a courtly gesture, full of dignity. "Again my apologies for disturbing you, and my thanks for your comfort."

He went outside with McClintock and Fry and they crossed to the barn. Fry asked, "Did this bandit get away with anything this time?"

"Not on the train," McClintock said. "Dead-eye Dick here just upped and started the shootin'."

"While you was gettin' yourself hit on the head," Burkhauser said dryly.

Carl Fry finished saddling; he led the horses from the barn and McClintock tied on their blankets and put the rifles in boots. Elmer Fry said, "Sorry I had to throw down on you like I did when you come in, but how is a man to really know? Ain't that right?"

"Don't give it another thought," McClintock told him. "You want me to give you a boost to the saddle, Finley?"

"I was ridin' while you was crawlin' on the floor and messin' your didies." He swung up, taking care not to bump his bandaged arm. "Fry, what's the best trail from here to Fort Parker?"

"Some old Comanche trails; they're all I ever heard about. Was I you I'd take one of the west forks of the San Jacinto, run it to the end then keep west until I hit the Brazos."

"Thank you," Burkhauser said and turned his horse. They left Fry's yard and Burkhauser made no attempt to pick up any sign of the bandit; he rode in a northwesterly direction, taking his time, sparing his horse.

For an hour McClintock said nothing, then he broke the silence. "Your arm givin' you trouble?"

"No more'n you'd expect. The pain killer makes it tolerable." He raised slightly in the saddle, either to shift position or to take a better look at the land; they were in a draw, following the natural configuration of it. On both sides they were bracketed by high hills. "We'll do better on the ridges. Especially when it gets daylight." He stopped and half turned in the saddle. "You been doin' any thinkin', Jim?"

"Some."

"See if I agree with it," Burkhauser invited.

"This fella knows you but you don't know him," McClintock said. "That makes for a mighty peculiar situation, don't it?"

"It does, I have to admit. However, I'm tellin' you the truth when I say that I've never seen him before." He fell silent a moment. "Still there's somethin' familiar about him, Jim. And don't tell me my memory's fadin' 'cause I'm gettin' old either; I remember every man I ever faced down, locked up, or shot. And he ain't none of them."

"Well, he sure likes to call out your name and beckon you on," McClintock said.

"Don't he though? Let's work our way to the ridge."

They left the draw and slowly made their way up the flank of hill, working slowly through patches of timber; it took them nearly two hours and when they reached the crest, Burkhauser slowly dismounted and squatted near a patch of cottonwoods. The wind husked along the ridge, rustling the branches and stirring the grass. He said, "If I had a pot and some coffee, I'd make some."

"You losin' your mind, Finley?" McClintock still sat his horse. "A fire would be a fine target, wouldn't it?"

"Get down a spell," Burkhauser said. "No sense in tuckerin' yourself out."

"Seems like one hell of a way to catch a man." He hesitated, then swung down and tied his horse.

Burkhauser lit a cigar and puffed it for a few minutes. "I put in fourteen years of service on the frontier with the cavalry. Ten more with the Rangers. In that time I guess I've pursued nearly every kind of varmint, two- and four-legged and not one damned one of 'em ever wanted to get caught. I've chased Indians clear into Mexico and as far north as Montana. And I've run renegade whites a heap farther. But Indian or white, they had one thing in common: they were bound and determined to make tracks and make 'em fast." He took his cigar out of his mouth. "Now here's a fella who wants to do just the opposite. He lets me know when he's goin' to hold up the train so I'll be on it. And now's he's in no real hurry at all." He chuckled softly. "Usin' my name at Fry's; now that was a nervy bit of business."

"Seems like you've got all the more reason for catchin' him."

"Sure, but I don't think I want to ride into an ambush in the dark."

McClintock straightened. "By God, now—"

"You're catchin' on," Burkhauser admitted. "Another ten or twelve years and you'll be able to think for yourself." He puffed gently on his cigar. "What other reason would he have for drawin' me a map?"

"Finley, how many men do you reckon promised to kill you someday?"

"Oh, somewhere near fifty. They never do though. By the time a man's spent eight or ten years in prison, his attitude changes. It's somethin' I never lost sleep over." He turned his head and looked at Jim McClintock. "What are you gettin' at? I've never seen this young fella before I tell you. If I had, I'd remember it."

"Well, he sure tried hard to put you up on a stick," McClintock said.

"This scalp ain't been hung yet. Spread your blankets and get a bit of sleep. I want to ride at sunup."

"You'll have a fever in the mornin'."

"We'll take it along then," Burkhauser said. "Fever comes from pain and infection. I'll take some more powder and won't feel any pain. Go on, get some sleep."

McClintock spread his blankets and rolled into them, using the crushed crown of his hat for a pillow. "Beats me why anyone would head for Fort Parker. That post hasn't been used for years. Most of the buildings are fallin' down and—"

"—there's no telegraph so I can wire ahead," Burkhauser said, stretching out. "Nothing between here and there except a lot of lonesome Texas."

"I'd like to know what his game was."

"If you knew every man's game, life wouldn't be very interestin'." He butted his cigar out carefully and settled back, cautiously cradling his injured arm in the most comfortable position.

McClintock spoke quietly. "Finley, do you hear from your kids?"

"Sure. Funny that you'd ask."

"It really ain't," McClintock said. "I was fourteen when I left home. Didn't go back or write for twelve years. When I got around to goin' back, ma was dead. Two brothers were dead, and my sister'd moved back East somewhere."

"Your pa?"

"He took off one day and was never heard from again. So I guess I like to see some kids keep in touch with their folks."

"Tom's practicin' medicine in Sacramento, California. Been there a year now and gettin' along fine. The two girls are married to ranchers up near the 'nations.' Wilson's workin' in a drugstore in Dallas. Roan and Miles are in the blacksmith business in Laramie, Wyoming."

"They've scattered some, ain't they?"

"Expected. The girls stayed near the home place. But you figure girls will do that more than likely. Why don't you shut up and go to sleep? Can't you keep in mind that I'm a sick man carryin' on in spite of my pain?"

They did not spend a good night for the horses kicked up a fuss at every small noise and McClintock kept waking up and toward dawn the pain in Burkhauser's arm began to bother him and he had to take a little water and some more of the powder Fry had given him. Dawn was a gray, miserable light and there were thick clouds in the sky that threatened to hold rain and the wind was booming along, picking up strength; it had swung around to the northwest and McClintock felt sure that it meant bad weather.

They had no coffee or a can to make it in, so they dipped into the bag of sandwiches the train crew had given them, and when they had eaten they mounted up and followed the ridge until noon. It was a gray, threatening day with a sky full of dirty clouds, and they moved toward the north, staying to the high ground where they could see great distances.

There was no sign of the bandit, no sign of movement anywhere. Below and a few miles to the west they saw an old wagon road winding through the valley. Burkhauser said, "That's the old fort road. Let's get out of this high country. Weather's going to break before nightfall and I want cover when it does." He pointed to a spot they could not yet see, a spot hidden by a low saddle of hills. "They used to cut wood in that locality. There are some buildings there, if they haven't fallen down."

McClintock's glance was quick; he had his hat pulled low over his eyes and had to ride with his head back in order to see. "Seems like someone else might figure—"

"Let's see if anyone takes a shot at us." He eased his horse down the slope, McClintock following him; they followed a twisting trail for the ground was uneven, rocky, with bare patches of loose earth that would have been the beginning of a slide if a horse missed his footing.

They reached the road and stopped a moment, then McClintock rode in a loose circle, studying the ground. "Buckboard's been through here recently. Two hours, maybe three on the out-side." He pointed. "Shod horse passed this way. Tracks are older though. I guess we're goin' in the right direction."

"Pickin' up company too," Burkhauser said. He shifted and caught his breath; his arm was still bothering him, for the powder had only taken the ragged edge off the pain. "We're wastin' time."

McClintock rode beside him and Burkhauser glanced at him but said nothing and McClintock was glad of that; he didn't want to argue now. He knew why they were following the road, deliberately hoping to draw fire; he felt now as Burkhauser did, that they were going to be ambushed, and this was a good place for it for the hills kept closing in, getting higher and steeper and he knew that a mile or so ahead the road would cut through a defile before opening into another broad valley.

Burkhauser kept swinging his head, watching the high places and the road ahead; he also took a look back now and then, but the land was silent except for some birds who wheeled and hawked at each other high on one side of the slope.

They came to a place in the road where the buckboard had stopped and the driver had relieved himself; McClintock picked up a stick and stirred the spot. "Thirty minutes. No more'n an hour."

He threw the stick away and then started when a dull boom set up an echo and rumble through the hills, slamming around, a sharper, explosive sound over a continuing rumble of sliding earth. Burkhauser shouted something and pointed ahead where the road bent sharply; a cloud of dust billowed and boiled a mile ahead of them.

Both started to ride forward at a gallop, crowding each other on the narrow road, then McClintock forged ahead and stayed there. He rounded the bend and saw the long slide of earth, like some huge mine tailing layering the hillside and covering the road. There was a pistol shot and then they saw the smashed buckboard; a stray boulder had bounded onto it, smashing it, and fatally injuring the horse. A man stood there, pistol in hand and he did not hear Burkhauser or McClintock come up; they were on him before he was aware of them and he started to raise his gun again, then dropped it when he saw that McClintock had him covered.

Dust powdered the man's dark suit and lay in the creases of his face; he flogged clouds of it off with his hat and wiped his face with a handkerchief. He looked at McClintock's pistol and eyes, and at Burkhauser, then a smile split the man's face.

"You must be the Rangers. For a minute there I thought—"

"Who the hell are you?" McClintock asked.

"Willard Beech. Special agent for the railroad."

"You're a long way from the tracks," McClintock pointed out. He got down and holstered his pistol only after he had seen Beech's wallet with his identification. "What happened here?"

Beech pointed to a scar on the hillside. "I'd say it was about twenty pounds of dynamite." He swung his arm to the north, along the ridge. "Our friend fired a rifle from there, a distance of about three hundred yards, I'd judge. While he judged his distance correctly there, he miscalculated my position for the explosion was a bit premature."

"I'd say it was close enough," Burkhauser said dryly. He walked over to Beech and looked at him; he was perhaps forty, short, and getting round in the stomach. He wore laced shoes and a derby and his celluloid collar had come unfastened. "Where did you come from, Mr. Beech?"

"Morgan Tanks." He saw the look on Burkhauser's face and went on to explain. "There'd been some trouble there a week ago, some railroad property stolen and I went out to look into it. I was waiting for the westbound, heard of the holdup, borrowed the horse and buckboard—" He spread his hands. "The rest is obvious."

"Not that obvious. Why were you on the Fort Parker road?"

"Elmer Fry told me. I was really only an hour or two behind you at the time. Must have passed you in the night." He looked from Burkhauser to McClintock. "I hope you don't think I'm interfering. There was an attempted holdup, which brings the matter into my province."

"That's a pretty dead horse, mister," McClintock pointed out. "What are you goin' to ride now?"

"I think I'll walk." He smiled. "Unless one of you wanted to ride double with a fellow peace officer."

"The best thing for you to do is to go back to Morgan Tanks or Fry's place," Burkhauser said. "You could make it in a couple days if you didn't poke along."

Willard Beech shook his head. He took off his derby and exposed a near hairless scalp. "As long as I'm going to walk, I'll do it in the direction of Fort Parker." His smile broadened. "The super wouldn't like it if I gave up the chase now. He's sensitive about duty and all that sort of thing. And a man has his reputation to think of, doesn't he?"

McClintock sighed. "I'll share the horse with you. Anything in that wreck you want to take along?"

"There's my duffle. Got some cooking uti—"

"Like a coffeepot?" Burkhauser asked.

"And some Arbuckle's camp grind."

McClintock got off his horse and walked back down the wagon road and began to gather wood for the fire. Beech stared at him, then said, "You're not going to build a fire now, are you? Here? Why, that fella with the rifle could—"

"Yep," Burkhauser said, dismounting. "And I'd just as soon get shot with a cup of coffee in my hand as not. There, there, now, don't take all this so serious like. I remember once when I was in the Army, and we chased these Comanches for three days. Just couldn't seem to catch 'em. Then I called a halt and we cooked a good meal and had some coffee and afterward we felt so good we caught the Indians, and took the whole passel back to the reservation." He clapped Willard Beech on the shoulder. "Now you just get out the pot and coffee and we'll brew some. You'll get a new slant on life afterward."

McClintock began to build the fire in the middle of the road; he got it going and added wood, then took the coffeepot from Beech and added water and coffee. While it was heating, he said, "Beech, it may make you feel a little better to know that this blast was meant for me." He glanced at Burkhauser. "There was no way of knowing I wouldn't be alone. The last look he got of Burkhauser was when he put the bullet in him. It might be that he figured I'd come on while you stayed behind, Finley."

"That could be."

"And he wouldn't know I had a horse. From the distance, he took you for me, Beech. We're both wearin' a dark suit. You see?"

"It hardly makes the situation more cheery," Beech said.

"You'll feel better after you've had coffee," Burkhauser insisted.

"Oh, to hell with the coffee!" Beech snapped.

Burkhauser smiled. "Got a temper, ain't he, Jim?"

"Yeah, but he'll feel better after he's had coffee."

Anger stained Beech's round face and his dark

mustache seemed to bristle. "Are you two crazy? I've heard a good deal about the Texas Rangers but—"

"Keep right on yellin', Mr. Beech," McClintock advised. He glanced at Burkhauser and rolled his eyes toward the crest of the bluff, then casually got up and walked over to where the horses were tied. Hidden by them, he reached under the neck and freed his rifle from the boot.

Burkhauser moved around Willard Beech and bent to the fire just as the echoes of a rifle shot banged around the hills. The bullet missed Burkhauser narrowly and sang off a rock and instantly Jim McClintock answered, firing several times rapidly.

Beech and Burkhauser ducked for cover and Burkhauser grabbed the coffeepot before someone knocked it over. McClintock was working his way up the rocky slope and the rifleman at the top was trying to get a clear shot at him but McClintock would only expose himself to fire or move, and then he did that in short jumps which didn't give the rifleman a chance for a clear, sighted shot.

Then there was a lull in the shooting. McClintock was a good hundred yards up the side of the draw, halfway to the top, kneeling in a small pocket and looking down toward Burkhauser who had a clear view of the rim. Finally Burkhauser got up and went back to the fire and put the pot on again and McClintock began to carefully work his way down. He came up to the fire and reloaded his rifle.

"Coffee's about ready," Burkhauser said.

"I could sure use a cup after that climbin'," McClintock admitted. He looked at Beech, who was just now coming from behind his cover. "Come on and have some coffee, Mr. Beech. Make a new man out of you."

"You might as well know that I think you're both crazy!"

"Now you shouldn't get excited like that," McClintock said softly. "It figures, don't it, that who ever triggered off the dynamite would have a look to see how good a job it did? Well, we'd have sure scared him off if we'd hid, wouldn't we? Come on now, have your coffee."

Beech came over to the fire, then he hunkered down and took the cup McClintock offered. He stared at it, then laughed. "If you'd have told me what you were doing, I wouldn't have had nerve enough to stand there and make a target of myself."

"Sure you would have," Burkhauser said. "Hell, man, it don't hurt to get scared once in a while. Keeps you from gettin' careless. Ain't that so, Jim?"

"Yeah. 'Course, I knew he'd miss the first shot. Shootin' down hill, at such a steep angle, a man just naturally pulls under the target." He grinned.

"Then too, I got the notion that he wasn't much of a shot from him wingin' Finley on the train. A good man with a handgun would have nailed his target dead center at that range."

"Boy I do like the way you figure these things out to protect me," Burkhauser said. "You got to remember, it's me he shoots at all the time. If you kept that in mind, I'd appreciate it."

"I'll give it some thought," McClintock promised. "Man, this is sure good coffee."

"You've got a one-track mind," Beech observed.

"Yeah," Burkhauser said, "he can only think of one thing at a time. And I guess it's just as well. A man can get to thinkin' about so many things that he gets confused, and you just can't rely on a confused man."

"You may have a point there," Beech said, then got up and walked over to the smashed, half-buried remains of his buckboard and began to salvage his gear. He had a pole tent, a huge roll of bedding, a .45-70 repeating rifle, a chest full of food and cooking utensils. A large duffle carried his spare clothing. Burkhauser and McClintock watched him stack these things, then McClintock said, "You've got enough there to winter out, Mr. Beech." He waved his hand to include the horses and all. "Borrowed horses, borrowed saddles, borrowed rifles, and borrowed coffee. We're sure poor, ain't we?"

Beech came back to the fire and looked at

them. "Gentlemen, I don't mean this unkindly, but I have never seen anyone more poorly equipped for pursuit."

"Oh, I wouldn't let that worry you none," Burkhauser said. "It's been my observation that a man just can't prepare himself for all the trouble he's liable to run into. So he just stays loose and makes the best of what he has. Let me illustrate what I mean. It wasn't long after Jim joined the Rangers that we found ourselves in Tascosa; we'd gone up there to look into some Indian trouble; they'd run off about eighty head of horses. Well, we got that settled all right and took a slow, easy ride south to Fort Bliss—it warn't more than four hundred miles. Well by golly, we were sittin' in the barbershop at Ysleta—I was gettin' a shave and Jim was waitin'—when these Apaches stormed through town and killed a few people on the street and crossed the Rio Grande into Mexico. Well, there we were with trouble on our hands and two tuckered horses out at the hitchrail. When I got out of the chair, Jim got his haircut and shave and I took a bath. Afterward we had supper in a little Mexican place; I remember it because they were the best chilibeans I ever ate."

"They sure were good," Jim McClintock said.

"Afterward we filled our canteens from the town pump, got on our horses and crossed the river to Mexico. Jim and I didn't have thirty cartridges between us. Our pants were out at the knees and the only two blankets we had were so full of sand fleas you could hardly sleep in 'em. You might say that we weren't equipped to chase fifteen Apaches into Mexico. Well, we dogged their trail for over a hundred miles through the wildest damned country you ever saw. Any man with an ounce of brains would have turned back and the Apaches figured that, but we lived on raw rattlesnake, drank water we squeezed out of wet sand, and we caught up with 'em on the north bank of the Rio de Santa. Killed six in that fight." He glanced at Jim McClintock. "He forgot to duck and took an arrow in the thigh. Gettin' that out took an hour or so, and it wasn't until we got to the Sierra Madres that we caught up with 'em. I tell you, Mr. Beech, a more ragged bunch of Indians you never saw. We opened up, killed one more and wounded two and the others gave up. Two weeks later we were back in Ysleta. There was a trial, the leader was hung and the rest packed back to the reservation in Arizona. And you know, that stupid Indian agent at San Carlos didn't know these bucks had broke from the reservation." He shook his head and laughed softly. "In all my service, Army and Rangers, I can't say that once I was properly equipped for the job I had to do. Usually a man just doesn't have men to go around, or some other damned thing. You see how it is?"

"Yes, I see, although I've never experienced—well, that type of adventure."

"If you're goin' to come along with us," McClintock said, "you'll take the grub, the coffeepot and skillet, and your weapons. We'll spell each other ridin' and walkin' to save the horse."

"I'm not going to head back to Morgan Tanks," Beech said. "I don't know as I'm as tough as you, but if I fall down, you just jerk me to my feet."

"Time to go," Burkhauser said and slowly got up, taking care not to jar his arm. Beech hurriedly threw together what he wanted, using the duffle because it had a canvas carrying strap; he slung this over his shoulder, picked up his rifle and spare cartridge belt, and mounted behind Jim McClintock.

They carefully picked their way over the rubble blocking the trail and slid down the other side to reach the road. Far ahead a dust smudge rose and vanished in the wind. Burkhauser pointed and said, "He's not very far ahead. But I guess he don't want to be."

In the distant hills, rain streaked from the dark clouds; they watched it march toward them across the valley floor. Will Beech said, "And I left my poncho behind."

"Good thing," McClintock said. "I'd have taken it away from you because I'm the selfish, jealous kind who can't stand to see anyone comfortable while I ain't."

"He'll be soaked before we are," Burkhauser said. "We'll make Fort Parker by nightfall."

"To what kind of a reception?" McClintock asked.

"Don't know, but likely excitin' as a mouse set loose in church," Burkhauser suggested. He turned in the saddle and looked at Beech. "Have you looked into these train holdups?"

"All of them. Same man; we're sure of that. But no identification. He has an accomplice. Makes a clean getaway. The railroad's pretty tired of it. Unless he's caught every young hoodlum in Texas is going to think he's Jesse James. It's not hard to start a rash of robberies."

"Not easy to stop 'em either," McClintock said. "This fella's had Finley goin' in circles. He even gets an invite to attend the holdup. Now that's real class."

The rain hit them a few minutes later, a few large drops at first, then a steady pelting that soaked them to the skin. Water cascaded from their hats and made the saddles soggy and beat the grass down; the horses lowered their heads and kept walking, following the old wagon road to Fort Parker.

McClintock, riding along with his own thoughts, wondered just what was waiting for them at Fort Parker. The place was deserted, out of the way, rarely visited by anyone, yet they were being led there as though they were on a string. He suspected that there was a trap to be sprung and he didn't like it, but he knew the only way to find out about it was to walk into it and trust to luck to get out of it.

There wasn't any doubt that Burkhauser was the target; McClintock didn't know why and he was sure that Burkhauser didn't either but it didn't change the fact that he was. The first robbery had netted the bandit nearly three thousand dollars, an amount large enough to rate space on the front page of every newspaper in south Texas. And to make it the kind of a story newspaper editors yearn for, the bandit had thrown down a challenge to Finley Burkhauser. This was a name not unfamiliar in south Texas, and in other parts as well; the bandit's challenge was printed and the captain foamed at the mouth when he read it.

During the second robbery, while nineteen hundred dollars was being taken, the bandit made an insulting remark concerning Burkhauser's ability as a law officer and the newspaper editors played down the robbery and played up the challenge to the Texas Rangers. Burkhauser was relieved of all other duty and ordered to capture or kill this bandit. Victims of the robbery were talked to and a description of the bandit was posted in every sheriff's office and Ranger camp from the Rio Grande to the Arkansas border, but nothing turned up.

After the third robbery, newspaper editors began to ask why no arrests were being made. The Liberty weekly ran a half-page paid letter addressed to Finley Burkhauser; it had been written by the bandit, mailed to the paper, along with the money to run it. Burkhauser established himself in the hotel at Liberty; he could do nothing else since the bandit had insultingly suggested that since the Ranger had neither the wit nor gumption to catch him without help, he would be invited to attend the next robbery, where and when it took place.

All this McClintock knew before he got on the eastbound to join Burkhauser, and he supposed to some it would seem that Burkhauser was yelling for help, but McClintock knew it wasn't that at all. The old man was being pulled into something deep, something he had to wade into to find out about, and he wanted someone who could get out in case he didn't make it.

That's why they were slogging along in the rain, heading for Fort Parker, with the rider ahead beckoning like a lifted hand. In Jim McClintock's mind, the last train robbery had already taken place; the bandit was getting what he wanted all along, Finley Burkhauser.

The bandit had played three hands, built the pot to a size where it couldn't be ignored. Now he was playing out the last hand and the old man was right in there with his chips.

Burkhauser was known as a man who called every hand, bluff or not.

And McClintock knew this was no bluff.

THREE

The rain fell steadily for the remainder of the day and darkness started to come early; they reached the river crossing and the water was rising a little; by the same time tomorrow it would be bursting the banks. Burkhauser led the way for the crossing was shallow, the water rising only to his stirrups, and when they reached the other side they immediately entered a rolling, wooded area.

"Cabins about a mile ahead," he said. "Army wood-cutting details used to camp here."

"All I hope," Will Beech said, "is that some kind of a roof remains." He turned and looked at the dreary back trail. "I would also like assurance that there is no present tenant who has the distasteful habit of setting off dynamite charges. I suppose that's really asking too much."

"I expect we'll have it to ourselves," Burkhauser said. "He'll be waitin' for us at Fort Parker. That's the plan, gents, and we've come too far now for it to be changed."

The darkness was gathering when they found what remained of the Army's wood-cutting outpost. The corral was in poor repair and the roof of the long barracks and wagon shed had fallen in. But the cabin which once housed the officers had been more stoutly built and appeared sound although some of the chinking was missing from the walls.

They stopped three hundred yards away and McClintock and Will Beech dismounted. McClintock said, "We'll take our look around afoot. If it's clear, we'll signal you." They left him, splitting to circle from opposite sides. Beech looked over the outbuildings and went through them carefully while McClintock approached the cabin. He kicked the door open and went inside, found it empty, and signaled for Burkhauser to come up with the horses. Beech took them, after Burkhauser dismounted and led them to the corral, tying them there behind the old barn where they would not be easily seen from the trail.

The cabin was full of the strong odors of mildew and McClintock rummaged around, found a box of old candles and put a match to one, melting wax onto the table to hold it up.

Some furniture remained, old chairs with the leather-laced bottoms brittle and rotting. There was no food, but there was wood for the fireplace and some rusty pans hanging from hooks imbedded in the mortar.

"Kind of cozy," Burkhauser said. "Well, I guess we could have a fire. We'll stand watches. The old barracks is the best place, I guess."

McClintock took a large pocket knife from his hip pocket, opened it and made shavings to start the fire. He got it going, fed small pieces of wood until the blaze would support some of the split logs. Heat began to push back into the room and they backed up to the fire and tried to steam dry. After soaking up a little heat, they took off their coats and vests and hung them near the fire on chair backs, and McClintock made the coffee and sliced a pound of bacon in Beech's frying pan.

"I don't want to sound like the worrying kind," Will Beech said, "but a man could be trapped in here."

"Oh, I guess once he could," Burkhauser admitted, "but not any more. A couple of men could push through the logs on the back wall easy enough if they had to. However, it ain't one of my worries. But if it eases your mind, Mr. Beech, you might take your rifle and go across the yard to the barracks and post yourself there. Jim will eat and as soon as he's finished, he'll relieve you so you can eat and dry out."

"That sounds all right to me." He picked up his coat and slipped into it, hefted his rifle and went outside.

Burkhauser said, "Nice fella. Green, but nice." He glanced at the fire. "Better turn that bacon, Jim. You know how I like it done just right."

"Then you ought to try doin' it yourself."

"Now let's not be touchy," Burkhauser cautioned. "I just like to see a man learnin' a trade, that's all." He dipped into his pocket for the small, folded package of powders; he had taken great care to keep it dry. He put some on his tongue, made a face, and rinsed it down with water from the canteen. "Why is it that all the stuff that's good for you tastes so bad?"

In Beech's food sack, McClintock found a small can of sourdough starter, some flour and salt, and he made pancakes in the skillet after the bacon had cooked. Working near the fire had pretty well dried out his clothes so he ate, drank some coffee, picked up his gun and went across the yard to relieve Beech.

After Burkhauser had eaten he stretched out on the floor and slept. Beech tried it and couldn't; the sound of mice moving around bothered him and he kept sitting up and cocking his head at the slightest sound. Around eleven o'clock, he got up and went out to spell Jim McClintock.

The fire was down so McClintock added some more wood before settling in his blankets. He moved quietly, lest he disturb Burkhauser, then the old man surprised him by speaking softly. "Beech all right?"

"He looked all right to me. Man, that fire feels good."

"You find a dry spot out there?"

"It's all right. A little chilly, but there's enough

roof on the west end to keep the rain out and still give you a good look at the yard and the back trail." He got up and put on some more coffee.

"You're sure a great coffee drinker, ain't you? If I'm asleep when it's done, wake me and I'll have a cup." He coughed gently and groaned when it hurt his arm.

McClintock's attention sharpened. "That ain't makin' pus, is it?"

"It's all right." He held up his hand. "I looked. Don't you think I care? It's just sore and will be for another ten days or so. Between you and me, I'm thankful the bullet didn't break a bone. That makes it pure hell, you know." He stirred in his blankets. "I remember a time on the San Saba—I was in the Army at the time and—" He closed his mouth when McClintock held up his hand.

"Think I heard a horse."

"You heard the rain on the roof."

"I tell you I—"

Will Beech yelled from out in the yard, and McClintock jumped up and drew his pistol from under his coat. Burkhauser rose from his blankets and said, "Take it easy. Let him handle it, damn it."

"He may be in—"

"He can handle it," Burkhauser said. He moved to the door and opened it. Beech was in the yard, with a rider who stood motionless under the railroad detective's gun.

They came on toward the cabin, the rider easing the horse in close; Beech was a few yards behind, in a position to shoot if the rider made the wrong move. The darkness was dense, yet a strong moon seemed to filter light through the rain clouds; visibility was fair for nearly a hundred yards, so good that the rider didn't have a chance to cross the clearing unobserved.

Burkhauser threw open the door. "Just step inside and don't do anything foolish with your hands," he said. "Jim, light the candle."

The rider dismounted and walked slowly toward the cabin door. McClintock could see that he was slender and rather small and carried no side arms. He wore a long leather coat and a hat misshapen by the rain. Beech put the muzzle of the rifle in the rider's back and pushed him inside, and McClintock reached out and jerked off the wet hat and long brown hair cascaded damply past the rider's shoulders.

McClintock's jaw went slack and he stared foolishly, then said, "May, for God's sake—" He let it trail off and regained his composure. "All right, May, stand over there by the fire. Will, take her horse around with the others then come on in."

The girl moved over by the fire and stood there, hands behind her. Water dripped from her coat to the plank floor and the candlelight made sharp shadows and highlights on her face. She was in her mid-twenties, taller than the average woman, and completely unafraid.

She said, "I'm sorry, Jim, but when I learned you'd be on the train, I just couldn't let you be killed." Her glance went to Finley Burkhauser. "Do you have to look at me like that?"

"How do you look at a woman who's made a sucker out of a man?" Burkhauser asked.

The girl looked at Jim McClintock. "What we had was real, Jim. Can't you believe that?"

"There seem to be a lot of lies between us, May. I don't know what to believe." He shook his head. "You're the last person I expected to see, May."

Burkhauser said, "Take off your coat and dry off, girl. You look like a scalded shoat." He waved his hand at the blankets on the floor. "If you want to dry your clothes, you can use one of those to wrap yourself in."

Will Beech came in and flogged water from his hat. The girl said, "Was that your rig that got caught in the slide? Too bad about your horse. He looked like a nice one."

"Your concern is touching," Beech said. "What's your name?"

"Her name is May," Burkhauser said dryly, "and she's Jim's girlfriend."

"Now listen here!" Beech snapped. "I'm in no

frame of mind to put up with your damned jokes!"

"No joke," Burkhauser said. "Put some slack in your rope. She rode in here for a reason. She knew we were here. She knew Jim was going to recognize her, and she knew what it was going to cost her." He looked at the girl. "Would you like some coffee?"

"Yes," she said, "that would be nice."

McClintock got her a cup and brought it to her and she put her hands over his and held them, looking beseechingly into his eyes. "Jim, what I felt for you was not a lie. If I hadn't loved you, really loved you, do you think I'd be here now?"

"I'm really not sure why you're here, May," McClintock said and turned away from her. She took off her coat and stood close to the fire and steam rose from her flannel shirt and denim jeans.

Will Beech kept making faces and blowing out his breath; he was full of impatience and he kept looking at Burkhauser, who seemed quite unconcerned.

Finally Beech said, "Adding two and two, I take it that you provided the horses after the train was jumped."

"Yes."

"The other times too?"

"Yes, the others too." She looked at Jim McClintock. "Then I'd meet you in Laredo and somehow I could forget what I'd done, and why I'd done it."

"And just why did you do it?" Beech asked.

"Don't push," Burkhauser said easily. "Let her tell it her own way and in her own time." He patted his inner pockets for a cigar and found his last one, a bit soggy and bent, but smokeable. "You'll get your answers, Will. It doesn't matter if she tells you or not; you'll get it all figured out in time." He smiled behind a cloud of tobacco smoke. "You've been doggin' our trail since we left Fry's place. When we bedded down on the ridge you weren't more'n two hundred yards off. That's what made the horses nervous and uneasy. Jim, why don't you cook somethin' for the lady? It's been cold camp all the way for her." He looked steadily at her and shook his head. "Think before you let your pride speak out. We've got bacon and Jim makes a fine pancake, if he don't burn it."

She nodded briefly. "If you'll let me go to the corner, I'd like to use that blanket and get out of these wet clothes."

"Remember I've got a gun on you," Beech said.

"Oh, put that down," Burkhauser said gently. "One woman against three armed men? I think we can take a chance."

"It seems to me that you take too many."

"I take what I have to," Burkhauser admitted. He sat down on the edge of the table and it creaked under his weight. "I got a good look at the bandit; he ain't old enough to be your father. Husband? Brother?"

She spoke without turning around. "Does he have to be either?"

"A woman doesn't provide a getaway horse unless the man is something," Burkhauser said.

She had her soggy clothes off and she padded barefoot to the fire, the blanket wrapped tightly about her. "Brother," she said. "And pretty much of a fool." Her eyes held onto his. "He wants to kill you bad, but he doesn't dare to. That's a bad off way to be, ain't it?"

"I don't know," Burkhauser admitted. "I've never wanted to kill anybody. Not even the ones I had to kill. It kind of goes against your taste too, doesn't it?"

"What makes you say that?"

Burkhauser rolled the smoke around in his mouth then took it out and held it. "You're here. I don't think that was part of the plan. Was it?"

McClintock was kneeling by the fire, the bacon frying; he looked up at her and waited for her answer. She said, "No. I was supposed to ride back to Liberty." She fell silent a moment and then Jim McClintock handed her a tin plate with bacon on it; she ate with her fingers, closing her eyes at the flavor and goodness of it. He gave her some more coffee and she said, "Mr. Burkhauser, how long have you held hate for a man?"

"I can't say that I ever have. How long can you hold it?"

"All my life, I thought," she said. "It's different, talking about a thing and doing it, isn't it?"

He nodded. "Usually. Doin' it always involves little things you never figured on. You found that out, huh?"

Will Beech said, "Damn it, what's this all about?"

"I don't know," Burkhauser said, "but if you hang on you may find out. We all may. Careful there, Jim, you'll burn that pancake." He reached out to the fire and flicked ash off his cigar. "Are you goin' to ride into Fort Parker with us?"

"Don't go to Fort Parker," she said. "I came here to ask you not to go on."

"You want your brother to get away that bad?"

She shook her head. "He can take care of himself." She watched him, waited for him to say something, but he was through talking. McClintock gave her the pancake, sliding it from the skillet to her plate.

"No jam," he said.

"This will taste like cake," she told him and smiled; it was a warming thing, breaking the gauntness of her face. She rolled the pancake and ate some of it, being careful not to burn her mouth. Then she looked at Finley Burkhauser. "My name is May Spaniard. Does that mean anything to you? I was six when you put me and my brother on the train. Do you remember at all?"

Burkhauser's eyes drew together and he pursed his lips. "Jacob Spaniard—I remember him. Got ten years for killing that shoemaker in Tascosa." He fell silent for a moment. "A bad business. No reason for it except whiskey and a bad temper. Your ma, is she alive?"

"In Mexico," May Spaniard said. "We all live in Mexico now. Pa's waiting for you at Fort Parker. Harry's with him. Others too. Turn back now; I'm not going to tell you that again."

"You haven't told me why you said it at all," Burkhauser said.

"Because now that it's here it's no good," May said, her voice expressionless. "It's all past, done with. It's just no good."

"I knew you were headin' into a trap," McClintock said.

"Take it easy," Burkhauser advised. "If I was supposed to be dead it could have happened on the train, or when that dynamite went off. Harry Spaniard wouldn't have to lead me by the nose to Fort Parker to do it. It could have been an ambush anyplace." He looked steadily at May Spaniard. "So what does he want?"

"Ten years. Just what was taken from him."

"That ten years was payment for an innocent man's life whose only mistake was to forget to clinch a nail in the heel of your father's shoe,"

Burkhauser pointed out. "That shoemaker left a wife and three kids too. What's the price they're asking?"

"You don't have to tell me all those things!" she shouted. "Don't you think I know them?" She pulled herself under control. "The year Pa got out of prison he went to Mexico, prospecting. He struck it in the Sierra Madres and he bought land on the Rio Salado, a lot of land. There he's a *patrón*; everybody does what he says. Once you got there, you'd never get out, not until he let you go and now I don't think he ever intended to do that."

McClintock said, "It's a long way from here to the Rio Salado, girl. There are three of us and—"

"Three of you! He has a dozen men with him. And all of them have something they want to collect from Finley Burkhauser." She finished eating and put the plate aside. "I can't go back now. When you don't show up at Fort Parker, Pa will figure out what happened. But it's not right, no matter how long I thought it was." She looked at Burkhauser. "You just can't teach someone else to hate, no matter how hard you try, can you?"

Will Beech blew out a long breath. "Burkhauser, you're not going to believe her, are you?"

"Why not? It's true," Burkhauser said. He threw his cigar in the fire. "Someone had to come back and make good their threat, didn't they, Jim? It just figures that way, doesn't it?" He adjusted his sling to make his wounded arm more comfortable. "A man's always in pursuit of somethin', isn't he? A gambler spends his life after money. Some men pursue happiness or power, or just peace. Look at you and me, Jim. We've spent our years in as relentless a business as a man can find, pursuing other men. Can you think of the trackless miles we've traveled with one goal in mind, to find that man and bring him back? Wouldn't you think that was dedication?" He shrugged. "Yes, I believe that Jacob Spaniard is after me. I believe he's carried his hate for twenty years. He could carry it another twenty and I'd believe it was possible." He glanced at the girl. "Who's with him?"

"Barney Rowland, Pete Tanner, and Harry Scanlon," she said.

Jim McClintock whistled softly. "Now there's three of a kind. I'd hate to have to bury the men they've killed, the ones the law knows about."

"You arrested these men, Burkhauser?"

McClintock laughed. "You could say that. Rowland he chased clean to Montana to shoot it out. Tanner ran for Mexico, and was caught there. Scanlon he caught in El Paso." He looked at Finley Burkhauser. "I think she's right. We shouldn't go on to Fort Parker."

"What do you want me to do?" Burkhauser

asked. "Jim, you know me as well as any man. What can I do? I've spent a lifetime being one way and now, because I've been caught between a rock and a hard place I've got to change?" He arched an eyebrow and pushed wrinkles into his forehead. "Come dawn we'll move on to Fort Parker."

"If you do that," Will Beech said, "you'll be throwing the girl away. Like she said, she can't go back now. Burkhauser, forget just once that you're a great man hunter. Forget about that badge you wear. It's the right thing to do."

"A man can't always do what's right, Will." He turned his head and looked at May Spaniard. "If I turn back, I'll do so only to get more men. Fort Parker is a long way from Mexico, girl. How's Jacob going to get back?"

"If I told you that you'd have a company of Rangers waiting for him," she said. "You know I can't tell you that. And I won't tell you. Already I've gone against him, but it's as far as I'll go." She watched him as though waiting for his argument, but he gave her none. She gathered her dry clothes from the back of the chair. "I did what I came here to do, so I'll be leaving. But I want to tell you that you're just as relentless a man as my father, Mr. Burkhauser. You'll use your gun just as quick. The only difference is that you don't hurt innocent people. You act for people, not against them." She let a small smile warp her lips into a bow. "I don't think you know how many years it took me to see that."

She went to the corner and dressed and Burkhauser clung to a thoughtful silence. Will Beech opened his mouth to speak, but Jim McClintock shook his head and that way held him silent. The rain drooled from the eaves and the fire cracked and threw sparks. May Spaniard, dressed now, brought the blanket back and folded it neatly. "I want to tell you about my home, Mr. Burkhauser; we have twenty rooms and servants to wait on us; it's everything anyone could want. The ranch is so large that a man on a fast horse can barely ride across it from sunrise to sunset. There are a hundred riders on my father's payroll and fifteen *pistoleros* see that my father's word is always obeyed. Let him go back there, Mr. Burkhauser. Let him go back, angry, and disappointed, but let him go. Is that so much for me to ask?" She looked briefly at Jim McClintock. "When I first met him I told myself that it wasn't possible for me to love a man, but I had a choice. I could let you ride into this trap and perhaps have Jim killed, or I could come here, show myself, end it all between us, and keep him alive. I made my choice, Mr. Burkhauser."

The old man sighed, then nodded and spoke to McClintock. "Kill the fire and gather our gear; we're goin' back."

May Spaniard's eyes filled with tears and she put her arms around the old man and kissed him. Then she said, "When you put Harry and me on the train you gave us each a bag of candy. Do you remember?"

"Yes, I remember."

"Do you remember what you said? Never bite into rock candy. Let it melt slowly, and when you have trouble, put a piece in your mouth. When it's gone, your troubles will most likely be gone too. Harry ate his that day. I saved some of mine. There's one piece left, in the jewel box on my dresser. When I get home I'm going to eat it. Harry's always been full of trouble. I think mine is about to end."

McClintock said, "You can't go this way, May. Not without us talkin'."

Burkhauser nudged Beech and said, "Let's see to the horses."

After they went out, McClintock rolled a cigarette and lit it. "What about us, May? It just can't end."

"How can it go on, Jim?"

He shook his head sadly. "I don't know, but I just can't let you leave like this. I want to marry you, May. I guess I fell in love with you right off, when you smiled at me."

"Isn't it really better that it ends this way?" she asked. "I don't like it but it's better. Not easy. Not even good." She looked at him a moment then came into his arms and pressed herself against him. "Hold me a moment, Jim. Let me remember what it's like to have your arms around me. Then let me go. I have to go."

They stood for a moment, silently, then she pulled out of his arms and turned to the door. She went out quickly and ran across the soggy yard and got her horse; a moment later she rode out and Jim McClintock blew out the candle and stepped outside.

Burkhauser and Beech came up with the horses and the old man said, "A man never knows about tomorrow, Jim. That girl's made out of stout stuff; I wouldn't give up on her."

"Who the hell is?" McClintock asked and prepared to mount.

"She talked about you putting her on a train," Will Beech said. "I didn't understand that."

"Jacob's wife had no money, but some kin back East. I just put 'em on the train, that's all."

"And paid for the tickets out of your own pocket," McClintock suggested.

Burkhauser snorted. "What the hell, don't you think I could afford it?" He took hold of the pommel and labored himself into the saddle. "Let's get out of here while gettin's good. I believe that when a man makes up his mind about something, then he ought to do it."

Beech went inside to make sure the fire was out and that no gear had been left behind; he came out and spoke to Burkhauser. "I don't see why this is so hard to do. Hell, you're not the first man who ever quit a chase."

Burkhauser turned his horse and rode off a piece and McClintock said, "Will, do you know what quit means?"

"Why, sure. What kind of a question is that anyway?"

"Finley's never heard of it. Let me tell you somethin', Will. A man's reputation is his asset or his liability. There isn't an outlaw in Texas who doesn't know that once Finley gets on his trail he won't stop until he's caught him. And you want to know something else? That's the kind of reputation I want and I hope I have the guts to bring it about. Now let's go."

They rode out the remainder of that night; then the rain stopped just before dawn and the sun layered the land with a bright, deep orange and the sky turned to the palest of blues, marred only by scattered clouds. The sun climbed hot and good in the sky and by midmorning steam rose from the green hillsides and they raised Elmer Fry's place in the early afternoon.

Burkhauser wanted to return the saddles, but Fry would have none of it; he told Burkhauser to leave them with the depot agent at Morgan Tanks and they would be picked up the next time he came in for supplies. Fry's wife cooked a meal for them; they ate, thanked the man and rode on.

Morgan Tanks was not a town, yet it was more than a water stop for the Houston & Texas Central Railroad. There was one street, running parallel to the tracks, but a bit south. The depot, water tank, coal yard, and stationmaster's house crouched by the track and siding. There was a cattle loading yard and the shacks of the Mexican section hands and their families. Beyond, fronting the north and lining the short street stood a saloon with a rooming house next to it and a Mexican-American restaurant farther down. The last building was a general store.

They dismounted and tied up in front of the saloon and went inside. Burkhauser held up three fingers and the bartender set out the glasses. The bartender looked at Will Beech and said, "I didn't hear you drive up, Mr. Beech." He walked from behind the bar to the door and looked out. "Didn't think I heard your buckboard." He came back to his place. "You must be the Rangers that were on the train."

"And you," McClintock said, "must be the nosiest bartender in Texas."

Burkhauser patted the young man's arm and McClintock poured another drink and stared at the grain of the bar. "When's the next westbound due through?" Burkhauser asked.

"Late tonight," the bartender said. "You didn't catch the bandit, huh?"

"Yeah we did," McClintock said, "but he melted in the rain."

"Drink up and shut up," Burkhauser advised. "Get us a room, Jim. I'll go send a wire."

McClintock nodded. "Is there a place where a man can get a bath and a shave?"

"At the store. In back."

Burkhauser and Will Beech went out and McClintock finished his drink, then gave the bartender two dollars and got a key for upstairs. He walked the few doors down and went into the store; it was a clutter of clothing and hardware and groceries.

"A bath and a shave," McClintock said.

"Bath is a quarter. Use of the razor a dime," the owner said. "Soap's a nickel."

"Suppose I just buy the whole, grand package," McClintock suggested. "That's the kind of a fella I am, not in town a half day and I've spent a quarter."

"You'll have to wait a few minutes," the man said. "The tub's occupied. Look around the store if you like."

McClintock moved around the counters, intending to look, but he bought underwear, socks, another shirt, and a half-dozen cigars. He paid for these and waited, leaning against a counter, then the door to the back room opened and May Spaniard came out. She wore a clean dress and her hair was damp and when she looked at Jim McClintock her eyes opened in surprise, then she masked this and went out without saying a word.

He had his bath and shave and took his time about it, enjoying a cigar while he bladed his cheeks clean and trimmed his mustache. Then he dressed and went back to the saloon, taking the outside entrance to the second floor. He walked down a short hall and fitted the key to his door; he stopped as the door behind him opened and May Spaniard said, "Could I talk to you a moment?"

McClintock turned. "Sure."

"Inside?"

He stepped into her room and closed the door and she came into his arms, kissing him, holding onto him for a long moment. Then she stepped back and said, "I was going on, but then I saw Harry's horse tied down the street and I had to warn you, Jim."

"The damned fool wouldn't show himself here, would he?"

She shook her head. "You wouldn't think so, but Harry's wild. You can't predict what he'll do, Jim. He'll want to know why you and Burkhauser turned back. What can I tell him? I never could lie to him." She bit her lower lip. "Jim, can't you arrest me?"

"I don't know. Have to ask Finley?" He scratched the back of his neck and gnawed on his cigar. "You don't want to go back, May?"

"You know I don't."

"Burkhauser's wiring ahead. Captain Fuller will likely meet us in Houston." He took the cigar from his mouth and held it. "May, if Harry shows himself, and I saw him, I'd have to take him in."

"I know that."

"He held up three trains and tried to hold up a fourth. And if he's as wild as you say, he's apt to start shooting. I'll shoot back, May. It's my job, my sworn duty."

"I know, Jim."

"What I'm trying to say is, I don't want to kill your brother. So tell him to light out for Mexico. Tell him to stay there."

"The only rules Harry plays by are the ones he makes up," she said softly. "Jim, I know what I'm doing to you, tearing you down the middle. I don't want that. You do what you must do. I want you to do that." She turned him to the door. "Please go now."

He didn't argue; he stepped across the hall and into his own room.

He tested the bed; it was lumpy yet he found it comfortable when he stretched out on it. A man's step came down the hall; he thought it was Burkhauser, then there was a light tapping on May Spaniard's door. He heard it open, heard her gasp and say, "You damned fool, Ha—"

A meaty slap cut this off, then the door slammed shut and Jim McClintock came off the bed and lightly crossed to the door; he stood with his ear against it, listening before opening it onto the hall. He could hear a soft run of a man's voice behind May Spaniard's closed door and he unbuttoned his coat before putting his left hand on the knob. It turned smoothly, freely under his hand, then his lunge flung the door open.

Harry Spaniard jerked around and pulled his gun at the same time. He fired fast, from the hip and McClintock felt the bullet touch his neck; it thudded into the door frame behind him.

The spring holster under his left armpit popped as he freed his gun, thumbed back the hammer and let it drop as the front sight centered on Spaniard's breast bone. The .44 slug knocked him back and Spaniard triggered his second shot at McClintock's feet, then he dropped the gun and fell on it, twitching his feet a few times before being completely still.

The shooting attracted the bartender and Finley Burkhauser; they burst into the room and then Burkhauser pushed the bartender outside and closed the door. He saw the red welt on McClintock's neck where the bullet had just touched him, then knelt and rolled Harry Spaniard over on his back.

May was backed to the wall, both hands over her mouth, but she was not crying. Slowly she took her hands away and came over to where McClintock stood; she looked at him for a moment, then gently laid her hand on his arm and turned her head away.

"Don't say you're sorry," she said. "What else was there to do? He was such a fool. So sure no one could ever really touch him."

"What made him come here?" Burkhauser asked. "A man ought to have more sense than to—"

She turned and looked at him. "Does that really come into it? Do you think he thought of that?" She shook her head. "I hope this finishes it. You can close your case now, can't you, Mr. Burkhauser?"

"Yes. I'll put it in my report that he got into your room for the purpose of hiding." He took off his hat and ran his fingers through his thick hair. "Of course it's in my mind that a man is living who hates me enough to want to kill me."

"He did that when you didn't know about it," she said. "It didn't bother you then. Don't let it now."

"But it does," Burkhauser said. "You'll tell him what happened?"

"Yes," she said. "I'll try to make him understand."

"But he won't," McClintock said.

She shook her head. "No, he won't. You can't expect him to. He's right and everyone else is wrong. To some people, the world is just upside down all the time."

McClintock said, "I'll go get the bartender and we'll get him out of here."

"No, I'll attend to it," Burkhauser said and went out, closing the door.

For a moment the silence ran deep, then May Spaniard said, "I don't suppose I'll see you again, will I?"

"Do you really think that?"

She looked at him steadily and he studied the color of her eyes and the soft turn of her lips. "What ever Burkhauser takes it in his head to do, don't be a fool and do it too, Jim." She put her palms lightly on his chest and he could feel the warmth of her touch through his shirt. "That's what I meant when I said I'd never see you again; I'll be in Mexico and you'll be here, in Texas. I won't come back and I don't want you to come south."

He laughed softly. "Hell, you don't think Finley would—"

"I've lived all my life with relentless men, Jim. Don't tell me what they'll do. I already know."

Burkhauser and the bartender came down the hall; they had another man with them, a Mexican section hand, and Burkhauser opened the door and inclined his head toward the dead man and the bartender and the Mexican picked him up and carried him out.

"I'll see that there's a marker put up," Burkhauser said. He waited for her to say something, but she held to a silence. He looked at Jim McClintock. "Comin'."

"In a minute."

"Oh," Burkhauser said and went out, shutting the door.

FOUR

Captain George Fuller met them at the Empire Hotel; he was a small man with a dark complexion and a bristling mustache; he reminded Jim McClintock of a game cock spoiling for a fight. Fuller had dinner for three brought to his room; they ate and enjoyed coffee and cigars before he brought the conversation around to the dead bandit.

His penetrating glance settled on Jim McClintock, and he said, "Other than blind, staggering luck, you'd never have caught him, would you?"

"I guess that's as good a way of puttin' it as any," McClintock admitted.

Burkhauser frowned. "I don't see as our effort was entirely wasted, Captain."

"Oh, I didn't mean that," Fuller said quickly; he even smiled briefly. "I was just pointing up the fact that a man in our business has to rely on luck more than—well, anything else." He studied his cigar. "We have an enviable record, gentlemen, but I wonder sometimes just what it is. Do we pursue a man logically, or do we just keep at it until our paths cross? It's a good question, isn't it?"

"It's a fact," Burkhauser said, "that if Spaniard hadn't pulled that fool stunt and came back to Morgan Tanks—"

"—and I hadn't been across the hall," McClintock said, letting his smile grow. "Aw, come on, Finley, don't take it so hard. The case is closed so let's let it go at that."

"He's right," Fuller said. "Finley, we're well rid of this; the newspapers were making a big thing out of this bandit; it wasn't doing any good at all. Now he's dead, killed in a gun fight with a Texas Ranger. That'll look good in print, Finley. It makes a man think before he breaks the law." Fuller rolled his cigar between his fingers. "You never did find out who Spaniard had working with him, did you?"

Burkhauser shook his head. "Cold trail there, Captain. By the time we got back to Morgan Tanks—"

"Yes, I know. Well, we can't have everything, can we?" He chuckled softly. "This girl, the one Spaniard—"

"I figured a robbery motive," McClintock said quickly. "No other reason that either of us could see. Ain't that right, Finley?"

"That's about the size of it," Burkhauser said. "Anythin' else you want to talk about, Captain?"

"In a hurry to leave?"

"No, I just wanted to change the subject."

"To what?"

"Well, I'd like to take a couple months leave," Burkhauser said evenly. "I've been at it pretty hard these last few years and I thought I'd travel around a bit, see old friends, visit my kids; I've got grandchildren I've never even seen you know."

George Fuller's glance swung to McClintock. "I suppose you're tired too. Need some leave."

"Me? What makes you think that, Captain?"

"I figure you'll want to go to Mexico with this old fart." He laughed at their expressions. "I've got a memory too, Finley, and I have access to the records. The minute I got your wire and saw Spaniard's name, facts started to click. The trouble is, Finley, you've never given me my full due; I'm a very intelligent man. Not only that, I have a clerk who can find things for me. So I just lit one of my good cigars, leaned back, and thought about it awhile. It wasn't hard to come up with an answer. Jacob Spaniard went to Mexico as soon as he got out of prison, he and two other men. He still lives in Mexico, but nothing was ever heard of the two men who went with him." He shrugged his thin shoulders. "You add to those facts the business about the bandit baiting you personally and you get the idea that Jacob Spaniard is trying to reach out for something. Right?" He looked from one to the other. "Well, somebody better say something."

Burkhauser sat for a moment, his long legs

crossed, his hands idle on his knee. "George, there comes a time in his life where loose ends bother him. I'm goin' south of the Rio Grande."

"To find Jake Spaniard?"

"Yes."

"And do what?"

"I don't know, George. Whatever old men, and old enemies do." He looked at Jim McClintock. "And I want to go alone."

"And I've got my reasons for goin' along," McClintock said. "And don't give me a stupid argument about it." He stopped talking and got up to answer the light knock on the door. The clerk stood there, his manner apologetic.

"Sorry, sir, but there's a gent in the lobby who wants to see you and the other gentlemen." He handed McClintock a card; he read it and turned his head.

"Will Beech, the railroad investigator."

"Ask him up," Captain Fuller suggested.

McClintock sighed. "You heard the captain." He stood there, the door open while the clerk went down the stairs and a moment later Beech came up. He wore a clean suit and his hair was neatly plastered to his scalp, the center part very precise. He shook McClintock's hand and stepped in and was introduced to George Fuller, then invited to sit down.

Fuller said, "I was just about to grant leave to Mr. Burkhauser and Mr. McClintock so they could go to Mexico and look for Jake Spaniard. Now I don't suppose you'd be interested in going along."

For a moment Beech's eyes darted from man to man, then he studied his folded hands. "I thought the matter was closed. As far as the railroad is concerned—"

"Yes, yes, of course," Fuller said quickly. "We've closed the case too. But Burkhauser feels that a personal matter has developed. Since you were somewhat involved in this, Mr. Beech, I—"

McClintock laughed suddenly and turned to Beech. "Did you ever get that buckboard squared away with the division mana—"

"Are you trying to interrupt?" Fuller asked.

"Me, Captain? No, sir."

"Then don't change the subject," Fuller suggested. "Where were you exactly when Spaniard was shot?"

"Taking a bath in the station agent's tub."

Fuller's thick eyebrows went up. "A bath, Mr. Beech?"

"It's a habit I picked up from my mother, Captain. I heard the shots, three of them, two closely spaced, then the third a second later. By the time I got into my clothes and located the source, Sergeant Burkhauser and the saloon-keeper were carrying the dead man outside. McClintock was still with the deceased's sister."

"Ah," George Fuller said, like a long sigh, and McClintock put his face in his hand and sat that way and Burkhauser found the toes of his boots fascinating. Fuller let the silence stretch out, then he spoke softly. "Now aren't you ashamed, holding things out on me, your captain, a man who loves you like a brother?"

McClintock said, "Will, you're the blabbinest man I ever knew."

"What did I say?"

"Forget it," McClintock said wearily; he raised his eyes and looked at George Fuller. "All right, so you know why I want to go. She's worth saving, ain't she?"

Fuller put a finger in his ear and joggled it, as though trying to clear his hearing passages. "You, with a woman in Laredo?" Then his eyes widened. "Not the same one?"

Burkhauser laughed. "It was as much a surprise to Jim."

"Aw, cut it out," McClintock said. "Captain, May's a fine girl, and if I ever get her clear of this mess, I want to marry her." He puffed his cheeks. "This is a hell of a storm over nothin', the way I look at it."

"She provides the getaway horses and it's nothing?" Fuller asked.

"By God, she deserves better than she's got!" McClintock shouted. "Pure and simple, that's it!"

Beech said, "My, we do raise our voices around here, don't we?"

"Now I'm going to raise my voice a little," George Fuller said and McClintock straightened in his chair and Finley Burkhauser looked up. "I'm not even going to bother with three guesses as to who provided the getaway horse for Spaniard during this and other robberies. That's water under the bridge, for the time being. But I am very interested in something that's been in the files for nearly eight years. I'm talking about Cash Randolph and a man called Mushy. Randolph has a sister living in Laredo. Jim, I want you on the first available train. Talk to her, get all the facts you can about her brother, and wait at Ranger headquarters there." He switched his attention to Burkhauser. "Mushy was a horse wrangler around Hondo. Everybody knew him. Check that out and meet Jim at Laredo. These men joined Jake Spaniard and went to Mexico with him, but they never came back. We made inquiries some years back and even sent a man down there. You remember Ubanks, Finley. He was killed near Fort Ringgold three years ago. Ubanks found nothing except what the *rurales* thought; it was their opinion that both men had fallen into the hands of bandits and had been murdered for their clothes, mules and weapons. It's not an unlikely story, but it's not conclusive." He paused to light his dead

91

cigar. "You want to go to Mexico so bad, all right, you can go, but we'll do it right. By the time you're ready to leave, I'll have cut through some red tape so you can cross the border with the sanction and blessing of two governments."

McClintock grinned. "Boy, now just let me hear that the captain ain't the sweetest fella that ever—"

"All right!" Fuller said flatly. "You want to find Jake Spaniard, then I'll give you a long rope, something to pull you back with. Don't get the idea that it'll be any help to you. It won't. But it will give me an edge to send the Army in if you don't get back."

Burkhauser said, "Who did you say was the sweetest fella—"

"I take it all back," McClintock promised. "I never seen such a mean man."

"It seems damned funny to me to be making such a big fuss after eight years," Burkhauser said. "But I suppose those are the terms and a man either accepts them or gets no leave."

"You see right through me," Fuller admitted. "All right?"

"How the hell else can it be?" McClintock said. He looked at Will Beech. "I don't suppose you'd know when the westbound was due through, would you?"

"I'll loan you a time table," he said, "and I

might even ride as far as San Antonio, just for the company."

"This *is* my lucky day," McClintock said.

"Well, you've got your assignment," Fuller said. "Don't loaf around here in luxury."

"A cruel master, that's what you are," McClintock stated. "I just know I'll never make sergeant."

"You could make the stockade a lot easier," Fuller promised.

After McClintock and Will Beech left, George Fuller leaned back in his chair and laughed softly. "I signed his papers day before yesterday but I'll be damned if I'll tell him. Wait until he gets his first pay and finds the extra money. Then when he comes storming into the office, complaining because the clerks can't count, I'll tell him."

"You are," Burkhauser said dryly, "just bubblin' over with the milk of human kindness. What are you trying to do, get him out of the way for a few weeks?"

"What do you mean?"

"Sending him to Laredo to talk to Randolph's sister. Hell, it's all in the file, ain't it?"

Fuller pulled his eyes nearly closed. "Finley, I'm going to give it to you straight-haired; there are some things a man shouldn't do and one of them is to follow you to Mexico. Let's play this hand face up, Finley. You and I understand each other; we've known each other long enough, and disagreed often enough. Somewhere along the line of a man's life he's got to learn to let go. I had to learn it and it wasn't easy. I had to realize, to learn to live with the fact that I couldn't always win, that I couldn't make everything come out right. Now you're too old a man to change much so I've decided not to stop you. You want leave, then you can have it. But you've no right to take Jim McClintock with you. And you know he'd go because he likes you. Jim's the sticking kind, right to the last cartridge. I don't think you want to see him killed."

"That's right, I don't."

"Then let him get on the westbound for Laredo. I can guarantee you a two-week head start."

"George, I appreciate that."

"I suppose you do, but *I'd* appreciate it a lot more if you'd forget about Jake Spaniard."

"Don't you want to close the book on him?"

"Not that bad," Fuller said.

"What do you think Jake Spaniard is going to do when he finds out his son is dead?"

"I hope he's the kind who will cry about it, and forget revenge."

"He won't," Burkhauser said. "He's got Barney Rowland, Pete Tanner, and Harry Scanlon with him. If Jake wanted to forget, do you think the others would let him?" He shrugged his shoulders. "George, I know what it is to get something on your mind and not be able to put it down until it's done. It seems that all my life there's been Indians or renegades or outlaws that needed tendin' to, one way or another. And it's always seemed that I've been better suited to the job than the next man. George, we are what we're meant to be. I wouldn't care to say who decides these things, but it's decided. A man is smart not to fight it." He sat for a moment in silence. "George, did you ever see a couple of old bull buffalo have at it?"

"I've seen it. Never gave it much mind though."

"They're old, George. Old and tired and they've fought a hundred young bulls in their time, and every time it gets harder to win. They carry more scars now, and each time they take longer to heal. But the fight is still there, the knowledge, the will; they just lack the strength. So they put their heads together and paw the dust and after awhile they both back off, knowing it's all over, that this is the end of it. Jake Spaniard and I are a couple of old bulls, George. On opposite sides of the fence from the beginning. I'd had three or four run-ins with him before he killed the shoe-maker. Bested him every time; it was a shame he could never forget."

"Now it's got to be one more time."

"Yes, because he wants it. I never hunted him, George. Give me credit for that."

"I do, but will he fight or will he have it done?"

Burkhauser shrugged. "I think that if I can face him once more, he'll lower his head and paw the ground. Anyway, I'm goin' to Mexico to find out."

Jim McClintock and Will Beech got on the train for Laredo at eight thirty and found places in the chair car; the train was not crowded and they took window seats, sitting across from each other. The train hardly got into motion when a distinguished man with near white hair and a sixty dollar tie pin came down the aisle and took the window seat across from them.

Ahead of them, a baby wailed fretfully and a woman soothed it. The conductor made his way down the aisle, followed by three men; one of them paused across from McClintock and Beech and spoke to the well-dressed man. "Is this seat taken?"

"Not at all, sir," the man said and made room for the other to sit down.

The other two men came on, paused by them; they were middle-aged, dressed in wool suits and they wore them uncomfortably, as though dressing up was a chore they could barely tolerate. One of them smoked a cigar, against the rules; he gave McClintock the impression that he didn't think much of any rules.

He looked at McClintock's feet and said, "If you take those down I'll sit down."

"There are plenty of empty seats on the train," McClintock said. "Go someplace else and be comfortable."

The man puffed his cigar and looked at McClintock steadily; the other man started to move, but was checked with a hand motion. The well-dressed man across the aisle snapped his fingers, drawing McClintock's attention. "Give the gentlemen the seat." He let his glance drop briefly to the derby in his lap and McClintock followed the movement and saw the blunt barrel of a .44 barely peeking out.

"Now that's what I call a persuasive argument," he said, taking his feet down.

"What is?" Will Beech said, then saw the gun. "Oh," he said and took his feet down also. "You fellas really want the seat, huh?"

The two men sat down and one of them took a newspaper from his pocket and laid it in his lap; he slipped his hand and a .45 Colt under it and McClintock heard the gun being cocked. "That's not the friendliest gesture I've ever seen," he said. "What do you want?" Neither of the men spoke and McClintock looked across the aisle and the white-haired man smiled behind his dense mustache.

"They want to make sure that you get off the train when they do. That's not unreasonable, is it?"

"Just where are we getting off?" Beech asked.

"Laredo," the man said. "The point is, we'll get off together."

"You're goin' to keep a gun on us all the way to the border?" McClintock asked. "For ten hours?" He laughed gently. "You're as screwy as a wooden watch, friend."

"I think we'll manage," the man said. "But since we're going to be traveling companions, allow me to introduce your new friends. The gentleman with the cigar is Barney Rowland. The man holding his pistol under the newspaper is Pete Tanner. Pete is a little nervous about being in Texas. You see, when he left Huntsville, he did so without saying goodbye to the warden or getting the blessing of the state." He let his cold glance slide to Will Beech. "Just what is your occupation, little man?"

"Ladies foundation garments," Beech said dryly.

The man laughed and nodded to Barney Rowland. "He's a railroad dick. Pull their teeth."

Rowland snapped McClintock's pistol from the spring holster and tucked it under the seat. He felt of Beech's pockets and located the pistol belted to his waist; he slid this under the seat then leaned back. "They're gelded, Mr. Spaniard."

"Good." He took a cigar from a gold case and the man sitting across from him quickly struck a match. "It was very foolish of Harry to go back

98

to Morgan Tanks; I told him not to. But when you didn't show up at Fort Parker—" He spread his hands in an idle gesture. "Where's Burkhauser?"

"How the hell do I know?" McClintock said. "Do I look like his mother?"

Barney Rowland hit him in the mouth and when some of the other passengers heard it and looked around, he smiled and said, "Just a friendly argument. All right?" They thought it was because they went back to their own business and Rowland's expression turned hard. "Don't get smart with Mr. Spaniard. No one gets smart with Mr. Spaniard. Understand?"

"You have a way of drivin' home a point," McClintock said and wiped a trickle of blood from his lips.

"It will pay you to answer clearly any questions I ask," Spaniard said. "My son told me he put a bullet in Burkhauser's arm."

"He grazed him," McClintock said. "Not much to it." He let a smile grow. "Now I shot straighter. I got your son dead center, first shot."

A bleakness came into Jacob Spaniard's eyes and his face settled into an aged mask. "We'll talk about that when we get to my hacienda in Mexico. He was my only son. I had plans for him." He sat in reflective silence. "But I have some plans of my own. Before we cross the border I'll wire Burkhauser and tell him that I have you. He won't waste any time getting to me."

"If you want him so bad, why don't you invite him to step out in the street and shoot it out? He ain't very fast with a gun, you know. And he's had more bullets picked out of him than peppers in a stage station bowl of chilibeans. But I guess you know how the old man is; he goes down but he keeps on shootin'. More than one man learned that too late."

"Burkhauser will come to Mexico," Spaniard said softly. "Now I suggest that you rest. It's a long ride to the border."

The conductor came back and took the tickets; Spaniard was very pleasant about it and McClintock watched for a chance to jump Rowland or Tanner, but he never got it and the conductor went on, turning the coaloil lamps down as he moved down the aisle.

Beech leaned toward McClintock and spoke softly. "The girl did a lot of talking, didn't she?"

"What else could she do?" McClintock said.

Tanner said, "Shut up, you two."

"It's a private conversation," McClintock said. "Keep out of it." He cocked himself mentally, guessing what Tanner would do and when the man started out of his seat, McClintock pasted him on the point of the jaw, smashing him back.

Tanner fell to the floor unconscious and Jake Spaniard said, "Now what good do you think that did?"

"I just wanted to hit one of you," McClintock said.

"Pete will even that up. You can bet on it."

"With my hands held behind my back?"

"Likely. He's not very fair really. No sense of sportsmanship at all." He nodded to the man sitting across from him. "Get him back in the seat, Scanlon. I don't want someone coming down the aisle to trip over him."

Escape, McClintock knew, was a hope and little more; he knew from experience that it was possible for one law officer with his wits about him to escort three desperate men over a thousand miles of wild frontier, and do it afoot if he had to. With this knowledge he was certain that four alert men, one always awake, would see to it that neither he nor Will Beech got a chance to make a break for it.

This was an experience for Beech, and an outrage, to be taken prisoner aboard the very railroad that employed him. Yet he was a man who learned quickly and took his cue from Jim McClintock, being calm and unconcerned about it.

The coach was quiet; the passengers were asleep, and McClintock dozed in patches, saving his energy for the time he would need it. Finally he reached out and touched the side of the seat where Jacob Spaniard sat; the old man came awake instantly.

"Want to talk to you," McClintock said very softly. "Let me change seats."

"Be smart and don't make trouble," Spaniard said. "All right."

McClintock slid across the aisle and faced Spaniard. He said, "You're not what I pictured at all."

"What did you think?"

"Oh, I guess a four-day-old beard, and smelling of whiskey."

Spaniard laughed softly. "I've always been a tidy man, and at one time, a poor, tidy man. Ten years in Huntsville changed my luck. It put scars on my back from the floggings and a few knots where ribs were broken, but it changed my luck. Ten years of that will give a man a purpose in life, McClintock. And you'd better believe it."

"Like getting even?"

"No, I'm not fool enough to believe I can get even," Spaniard said. "Understand me now: nothing is going to bring back what those ten years cost me. But I can let Burkhauser know what it's like to be penned up. I'm a rich man, McClintock. Growing richer too. I have more land than any man can rightly use. On this land I've built something special. I've built two rooms of a prison, and a yard, exactly like my cell and the sweat box at Huntsville. In ten years I learned every crack in the wall, every rough irregularity of the floor. It's something I took with me, McClintock. Finley Burkhauser is going to relive my ten years, day by day, beating by beating. If he survives it as I did, he'll be set free at the border."

"And you don't call that gettin' even?"

"An education," Spaniard said.

"What have you got planned for me?"

"You want it straight?"

"That's what I asked for, didn't I?"

Spaniard hesitated. "Let me ask one question and give me a straight answer. The railroad dick, what did he have to do with my son's death?"

"Nothing," McClintock said. "He was taking a bath down the street when he was killed."

"I can have that checked."

"Check it then; it's the truth."

Spaniard nodded. "Now, I'll answer your question, McClintock. I've given it some thought and I've come up with the ideal solution. My land is vast and the *banditos* who roam Mexico know they are welcome to cross it, stay a few days, a week, and go on as they choose. You've had *bandito* troubles, McClintock; you know them, bold, desperate men with no mercy. I'm going to turn you loose on my land and let it be known that you are fair game. That way it can't really ever come back to me that I killed you, or even had you killed."

"Man, you've got a sweet disposition," McClintock said dryly.

"I consider every man's hand raised against me," Spaniard said evenly. "I show no consideration or mercy and ask for none. And I get along very well that way. Now go on back to your seat."

"Turn Will Beech loose. He has no part in this."

"Now I can't do that and you know it," Spaniard said. "Go back to your seat now. I won't tell you that again."

Each time the train labored up a grade, Jim McClintock watched for a chance, but he was given none. Three times the train stopped to take on coal and water and he hoped that Rowland or Tanner would grow lax, but they never did, and he was an hour out of Laredo when he realized that they just about had him across the border.

When the train finally pulled into the depot, Spaniard was in no hurry to get off; he let the other passengers go first, then Rowland and Tanner followed McClintock and Beech to the platform. Spaniard spoke pleasantly to the conductor, complimenting him on the line and promising to ride it again. McClintock felt like balking but the pressure of a gun muzzle in his back urged him on. Beech was a little way ahead and they stopped near some parked buggies. The

Mexican drivers got down and a half dozen mounted men waited nearby, crossed bandoliers of cartridges heavy on their velvet jackets.

"My personal *pistoleros*," Spaniard said. He spoke in rapid Spanish then got into one of the buggies and motioned for McClintock to get in with him. Rowland and Harry Scanlon sat facing them while Beech was loaded into the other rig.

They turned about and headed away from the depot, away from town, taking the road east that ran along the river toward the Spanish settlement. They passed through a crowded adobe village full of barking dogs and naked children, then stopped at the ferry; a Mexican woke and bowed, waving his hat across his body and Spaniard's rig was driven on. He gave Scanlon a piece of paper and said, "Go on back to town and send that to Ranger headquarters."

"What the hell, why bring me out here to walk back?"

"Because you're not very bright," Spaniard said. "If I'd given you this at the depot, you'd have sent it right away, before we were across the river. Now you'll have to walk back to town, and that'll take twenty minutes. By that time, I'll be across. It will take the telegrapher fifteen minutes to deliver the message to the captain at Fort McIntosh, and he will waste five minutes screaming like a wounded bear." Spaniard smiled pleasantly. "You may go now, Harry. And don't get drunk. It isn't safe for you."

"All right, Mr. Spaniard. You want me to get a horse when I'm through?"

"Unless you want to walk seventy miles." He waved at the ferryman, and they started to ease away from the shore, following the rope strung across the river.

McClintock said, "Scanlon got a drinkin' problem there?"

"Nothing he can't handle."

"A man with a problem can't really be trusted," McClintock pointed out. "He'll get drunk someday, at the wrong time and—"

"And then Scanlon will go into the hills with the *banditos*," Spaniard said gently. "It's a thought that will hold a man even when he has an intolerable thirst."

"Is that the way you rule, by fear?"

"What else is there that a man really respects?"

McClintock said, "I didn't see your daughter on the train." Spaniard slowly turned his head and stared at McClintock, then he said, "She'll be along. Don't speak of her again."

"What'll you do, pitch me in the river?"

"My daughter and my wife are held aloof from these matters of day-to-day survival," Spaniard said. "You've been warned; I won't repeat it."

"She wasn't so aloof that she couldn't provide the getaway horses for Harry."

"It was against my wishes," Spaniard said, "now I suggest you drop the subject."

"When I get ready," McClintock said.

Spaniard shrugged. "All right, Barney."

The man raised his gun to hit McClintock and he started down with it and suddenly McClintock whirled, grabbed his arms and threw him over his shoulder, out of the buggy and clear of the raft. Rowland hit the water and McClintock cut it in a dive a second behind him and Rowland never broke the surface; McClintock had him, dragged him down to the bottom and jammed his face in the mud, holding him there with his knee while he wrested the man's gun away from him.

Rowland sank deeper; his shoulders and upper arms were in the mud when he quit struggling and McClintock, lungs burning, broke the surface and gulped air. The ferry had stopped and the Mexican clung to the rope while on the Texas shore Pete Tanner levered his rifle.

McClintock flung a shot at him and dived again while bullets speckled the water. He swam under the raft, came up the other side and put his hands on it to come aboard. There he stopped and looked into the muzzle of Jake Spaniard's pistol, just inches from his face.

"Come aboard, McClintock. You'll catch cold swimming." He plucked the gun from McClintock's hand, then got into his rig while the Ranger pulled himself from the water and onto the raft. "Pull on," Spaniard said to the ferryman. He looked steadily at McClintock, who was sawing for wind. "I expect Barney is dead." He shrugged. "I rather thought he would be the minute you hit the water. You're being very expensive, McClintock. Barney's been with me a long time. A good man. I'll have to tell the *banditos* to take special pains with you. It is important that a man die very slowly."

FIVE

There was a pueblo on the Mexican side of the river; it stood some distance from the ferry landing, squat adobes separated by narrow streets; the largest buildings were the church and cantina built around the plaza. McClintock was forced to wait until the other carriage crossed, then there was an additional delay when Scanlon came back just as the ferry was leaving and it had to be pulled back to the Texas shore to pick him up. When they reached the Mexican shore, McClintock was ordered to dismount and stand with Beech to one side with Tanner and Scanlon partially blocking them from view on the Texas side. For a moment McClintock did not understand this, then he saw three mounted men approaching the crossing from the Laredo road and he recognized them as Texas Rangers.

Spaniard spoke softly, pleasantly. "Someone heard the shooting and reported it. One sound from either of you, one gesture, and there will be more shooting and they are too far away to save you."

The Rangers stopped and one of them swung down and walked to the edge of the ferry landing; he shielded his eyes with the flat of his hand

and looked across the river at Spaniard's party. He stood there for a moment, then turned back to his horse and mounted; they rode back, satisfied that the whole matter was out of their hands.

Will Beech let go a long breath and spoke softly to McClintock. "It makes a man feel funny just to stand here and—" He shook his head and let the rest trail off. "When you jumped Rowland I put you down for a goner."

"Shut up," Pete Tanner said, "you don't have to talk so much."

From the pueblo, a detail of mounted soldiers rode toward the crossing; they stopped a short distance away and the lieutenant came on. He dismounted and spoke cordially with Jake Spaniard and they lit cigars. Then the officer saw Jim McClintock and his eyes widened in surprise; he smiled and stepped over and offered his hand.

"I did not expect to see you in this party, señor. But a pleasant surprise nevertheless. I trust your visit is unofficial."

"McClintock is my guest," Spaniard said politely.

"Prisoner is the word," McClintock said. "Lieutenant Rivas, as an officer, you'll have to make a report of this."

"Making a report is dull work and it takes time," Spaniard said. He opened his purse and counted out some gold coins, handing them to Rivas. "See that you and your men enjoy yourselves at the cantina. I'm sorry we can't delay further, but I want to reach my hacienda by tomorrow night. You understand and pardon me?"

"Certainly," Rivas said, bowing, pocketing the money. He glanced at McClintock and rolled his eyes. "In Mexico, señor, there are many poor men. We get along the best we can." He smiled and went to his horse, mounted up, and took the detail back to the pueblo.

Jake Spaniard said, "Get in the other carriage, you two. Pete, Harry, you keep your eyes open. McClintock is a bold man who will take any chance he gets. Rowland found that out the hard way."

"He also owed me eighteen dollars," Scanlon said, punching Jim McClintock with the muzzle of his pistol, "and I'm going to take that out of your hide."

"You can do that when we reach the hacienda," Spaniard said. "Let's get moving."

They moved that day and the next across a vast, semi-arid desert, marching always toward the mountains in the distance which with each mile became larger, more forbidding. The first night they camped at a water hole used only by Indians and *banditos*; there was no road, only a trail, ruts worn into the hardpan earth.

Toward afternoon of the second day, there was, in the distance, a smudge where tall trees grew

111

and the flanks of the mountains started to rise in irregular bastions of rock and earth. As they drew closer, McClintock could make out what at first seemed to be a small village, then he saw that it was a huge hacienda, completely walled, with blockhouses at the four corners. Around the west and south side, small adobes clustered, like chicks huddled to a hen for warmth.

As they approached, a party of *pistoleros* rode out to meet them; some were Americans, but mostly they were Mexican; the leader was a tall young man with a shock of yellow hair and dangerous blue eyes. He dressed in white duck trousers and shirt and wore a pair of pearl-handled revolvers in the most ornately decorated holsters McClintock had ever seen. The man's saddle was burdened with silver. He wore silver conchos on his belt and smaller ones on the band of his hat, which was a huge dish-brimmed Mexican felt. His spurs had huge rowels with sharp edges and two tear-drop danglers to stop the wheel and make it cut.

Sweeping off his hat when he approached Spaniard's carriage, the man said, "You're some overdue."

"Do you worry about me, Stark?" He laughed and motioned for his driver to pull up abreast of the other buggy; Stark moved around to the other side. "I've brought a couple of guests, Stark." He nodded toward Willard Beech. "This is Mr.

Beech. He's a policeman for the Houston & Texas Central Railroad. When you lose your baggage, you go to Mr. Beech and through careful investigation, he recovers it. Now and then he may be called to put a drunk off the train. Say hello to Mr. Beech, Stark."

The young man smiled disarmingly, and extended his hand; Beech did the natural thing and Stark knocked him out of the buggy. Beech hit on his shoulders and rolled and Stark laughed and whirled his horse around and drove him into Beech as he was getting to his feet.

Jim McClintock said, "Try that with me, hardcase."

It stopped Stark like a hand on his chest; he turned the horse and came back to the buggy and looked at McClintock with his emotionless blue eyes. Spaniard laughed softly and said, "This is Jim McClintock, Stark. He shot my son to death at Morgan Tanks and drowned Barney Rowland in the river. Let me tell you about McClintock. He's a dangerous, desperate man who will take his chance when he gets it."

"You think I can't handle him?" Stark asked; he seemed insulted. Then his right hand left the reins and instantly his pistol was cocked and pointed at Jim McClintock. "Did you ever see the beat of that, mister?"

"That's movin' some," McClintock said casually, masking his shock and surprise; he had never seen a weapon produced for action with any more speed. "You're pretty good on the brag too, ain't you?"

"Put it away, Stark," Spaniard said. "He's not afraid of you."

"I can make him afraid."

Spaniard shook his head. "I'm saving him for the *banditos*." He reached out and patted Stark on the wrist. "Take four men and ride to the border. See that my daughter gets home safely."

Stark backed his horse and nodded; he wheeled and nearly knocked Beech down again, then gathered four men from his detail and returned to the hacienda for a carriage and provisions.

Beech got back into the rig; he was bleeding from a cut on the cheekbone and he moved stiffly as though his joints pained him. Jim McClintock looked at Jake Spaniard and said, "You make a lot of mistakes, mister."

"Since they don't bother me, why let them bother you?"

They moved on and when they approached the massive oak gates, they were muscled open by six Mexicans and the rigs passed through and into a huge three acre courtyard. The hacienda was shaded by huge trees and there was a deep well near it. At the base of the walls on the east, south, and west sides were adobes and McClintock could see that there was, within the walls, a small town.

"I see you appreciate my fortress," Spaniard

said; he had gotten down and came over to stand near the off wheel. "There is no convenience here that I lack. Blacksmith, saddlemaker—they are all here to serve me. It impresses you?"

"Like a scab on the end of a man's nose," McClintock said. "Do we get down now or sit here?"

"Get down," Spaniard said. He looked at Pete Tanner. "Lock them up. In a few days, a week perhaps, we'll be ready to let you run into the hills. That will be exciting, won't it?"

"Too bad you'll miss it."

"I saw it once," Spaniard said. "They've all got Yaqui blood. They take off a man's fingers a joint at a time. And that's only the beginning. It took this one man four days to die. He screamed until he had no voice at all." Will Beech closed his eyes and Spaniard laughed. "Already we've turned the little man's stomach, haven't we?"

They were locked in a small room next to the stable; there was a solid oak door and one window, high on the wall side, too high to reach from the cell and approachable only by climbing onto the roof and letting down to it.

There was straw on the floor and the filth left by former occupants; the door was slammed shut, bolted and locked. McClintock looked around and Beech slowly sat down and put his forehead on his knees. He sat that way for a time, then Jim McClintock said, "I wish I had a good cigar. How about you, Will?"

The man did not answer for a moment, then he said, "What do you want to talk to me for?"

"That's a funny damned question. What's the matter with you?"

Beech slowly raised his head and looked at McClintock. "I don't have any guts. Can't you tell?" He started to brush dust from his clothes and then gave it up. "It's hell for a man to think he's as good as the next and then find he's no man at all."

"Why, because Stark knocked you down with his horse?" He sat down in the straw and put his back to the wall. The cell was cool, full of dim light that would fade quickly to night in a few hours. "The trouble with you, Will, is that you ain't learned to bluff yet. Why, when I jumped in the river after Barney Rowland I was so scared I nearly wet my pants. And that Stark, now he'd raise the hair on a bald headed man. You've just got to learn not to let these things show. No sense in buildin' up the confidence of the other fella, now is there?"

"You don't lie worth a damn," Beech said.

Darkness came, and a meal of beans and water. Later the cell turned cold and they shivered for a while then paced up and down trying to keep warm. The arrival of the sun did no good at all and it was midday before any heat worked through the thick adobe.

That night they got another bowl of beans and some more water; it was a routine that went unbroken for a week. They were not taken out once and they selected a corner to use as a toilet and learned to tolerate the mounting odor.

Finally the door was unlocked and two Mexicans, heavily armed, motioned for them to come out in the sunlight. Across the square McClintock could see Spaniard seated on the porch of his hacienda. Stark was with him, and Tanner and Scanlon. The Mexicans took them across to the porch and Jake Spaniard looked at them carefully.

"You gentlemen are not very tidy," he said.

"Well," McClintock said, "the accommodations in your hotel really ain't what they should be. All right with you if we move into the stable?"

"I see you haven't lost your sense of humor," Spaniard remarked. "That's good because we have a very dull subject to discuss. It seems that you have a knack for making enemies, McClintock. On the train you hit Pete Tanner in the mouth, a very impolite thing to do since he was trying to be nice to you. Then you drowned poor Barney. He couldn't swim, you know. And now you've insulted Stark; he doesn't take kindly to that." He turned his head and looked at the pale-eyed *pistolero*. "How many men have you killed because they insulted you?"

"About twenty," Stark said.

"Well, I can't have either Stark or Pete kill you, McClintock, because I've promised you to the

117

banditos." He paused to draw on his cigar. "You see, tonight you'll be leaving us. Or in the morning at the latest." His glance went to Pete Tanner. "Take him apart."

McClintock was not set for Tanner's charge; he went back, rolling under the man's weight, then they broke and came erect. A crowd formed a distance from the porch and Tanner wiped his hands on his pants and came in, fists cocked; he struck McClintock on the cheekbone and drew blood but before he could get away, McClintock opened a cut over Tanner's right eye and mashed blood from the man's nose.

They clinched, like nails locking in a board and pounded each other in the body; it sounded like a full wine cask being thumped with the flat of the hand, then Tanner went down, rolled to his hands and knees and spat out a tooth. His mouth was bleeding badly and one eye was rapidly closing.

Jake Spaniard said, "Come on now, Pete, let's do better than that."

Tanner nodded and went in again, but somehow he never did do much better; McClintock's fists were like rocks and there was an outraged strength in the tall Texan that Tanner just couldn't meet. McClintock hammered Tanner's eyes and face, then he drove the wind out of the man and broke him completely with a smashing blow behind the ear.

Tanner fell in the dust and lay still and two Mexicans came forward and dragged him away.

Jake Spaniard continued to smoke his cigar; he seemed bored by it. McClintock's breath was coming hard and Stark unbuckled his gunbelt and laid it aside. His hat was handed to a servant and he stepped off the porch with his cigar still clenched between his teeth.

Will Beech shook off the hands that held him and said, "Without your pistols you look like some Dallas punk."

Stark slowly turned his head and looked at Beech. "What did you say?"

There was only the slightest tremor in Beech's voice, and it could be mistaken for held back rage. "I've thrown a hundred like you off trains because they didn't have their fare. Did you hear that all right?"

"I'm going to have to hurt you some," Stark said and changed his direction. He came up to Beech and flicked out his fist and McClintock closed his eyes, unable to watch. He waited for the smash of knuckles, then he heard a dull plop and opened his eyes.

Stark rolled to his hands and knees, spat out the mashed cigar and slowly got to his feet. His spurs made muted music as he moved in toward Beech; he seemed less casual now, less in a hurry. His fists were cocked and he shot out his left; Beech let it bounce off his shoulder, then he grabbed Stark by the front of the shirt, whirled, flung him over his shoulder and bounced him again in the dust.

This time Stark got more painfully to his feet and arched his back as though relieving some hurt. Jake Spaniard said, "All right, damn it, quit playing with him, Stark!"

McClintock laughed and said, "Yeah, you could get hurt playin' that way. You got your white pants all dirty, *pistolero*."

Will Beech suddenly hit Stark in the mouth and knocked him down. "Keep your attention on what you're doing," he said. He rubbed his skinned knuckles and managed a smile.

"Why don't you go on and tree him?" McClintock suggested. "Hell, without his pistols he's nothing. If you want to waste your time on him, go ahead."

Jake Spaniard's voice was a whip. "Get up, Stark!" He waited until the man obeyed, then he pointed to Will Beech. "You've been a poor guest, Mr. Beech, and I don't like that. I think you'll be better off, happier with your friend, McClintock."

"I was getting tired of that cell anyway," Beech said boastfully.

Spaniard waved to the Mexican guards. "Take them back and lock them up. They can leave together." He turned and looked at Stark and there was contempt on his face. "Go clean up. Wash and change your clothes. And take your damned guns with you. You may run into some little girl who'll kick you in the shins."

The heat in the *pistolero*'s face was a frightening

thing; he looked at McClintock and Beech and killed them with his glance. Then he snatched up his guns and stalked off the porch; a Mexican got in his way and he knocked him sprawling.

They were taken back to the cell and locked in; Beech sat down as though the strength had suddenly left his legs. McClintock said, "You jumped right into the pot, didn't you?"

"With both feet," Beech said. He raised his head and looked at Jim McClintock. "The way I figured it, Spaniard wasn't going to let me go anyway."

"That was some pretty fancy wrestlin'," McClintock admitted. "You had Stark kind of confused there. You learn that while workin' for the railroad?"

Will Beech turned his head. "In San Francisco. That's my home. We lived near a colony of Japanese; they had a school about four blocks from our house. Called it *jujitsu*." He laughed softly. "The young Japanese boys would take lessons there and somehow or another they let me learn too. It's been handy for throwing drunks off trains, like Stark said."

"Don't pay too much attention to what Stark says," McClintock advised. "The only answer he has goes *bang*. It's the only voice he has that's worth listenin' to." He squatted in the straw across from Will Beech. "You made him look pretty stupid out there. Like my old man used to tell me: you want to humble a man, point out to him his weakness. He knows he's got it and never did like it any."

"Stark certainly pointed up mine, didn't he?"

"Some room for argument there," McClintock said. He stretched out and laced his fingers behind his head. "Better get some rest, Will. You never know when the fun's goin' to start around here."

Beech fell silent for several minutes, then said, "Jim, I want you to promise me something."

"If I can."

"I'm not going to be much good to you once we get into the mountains. I want you to promise me you won't slow down for me."

"Now you go to hell," McClintock said softly, and turned over so he wouldn't have to talk any more.

Their meal came at nightfall, again beans and water; they ate with their fingers, dipping out of a common bowl. When they were through they stretched out and listened to the sounds within the walls; it sounded like any other town with a heavy Mexican population and around ten o'clock it grew very quiet.

McClintock slept and when he woke he sat up, keenly awake. He heard a slight tapping, metal on metal, and knew it was this slight sound that had wakened him. Then he stood up and looked at the high, barred window. May Spaniard was there, crouched against the bars.

"Jim?"

Beech woke; he sat up, saw what the situation was and said, "Stand on my back, Jim, but take your damned boots off first."

McClintock found that he could easily reach the window; he gripped the bars and May Spaniard laced her fingers around his. "Jim, I saw what happened in the yard. I was upstairs in Mother's room." She bent quickly and put her cheek against his fingers. "There was no way for me to get a gun; Father keeps them locked up. But I brought two knives." She slipped them through the bars, a pair of ten-inch hunting knives. McClintock dropped them to the straw and reached through the bars to grip her wrists.

"Go back, May, before you're found out."

"I will," she said. "But I had to see you. I just had to talk to you."

Beech said, "For gosh sakes, kiss her and be done with it. You're getting heavy."

McClintock put his hands to her face and held her. "May, in another time, another place—"

"I know," she said softly. "Jim, I love you." She quickly put her face against the bars and kissed him, then she wrenched herself away and moved along the roof, going back the way she came.

McClintock got down and Beech arched his back to ease the muscles. He fumbled in the dark for the knives and cut his finger accidentally and swore softly. "Like a razor," he said, handing one to McClintock.

Taking the lining of his coat, McClintock ripped it into thin strips and carefully wrapped the blade of the knife, then tied it to the calf of his leg before pulling on his boots.

"I'm wearing button shoes," Beech said.

McClintock had him undress to the waist, then he wrapped the other knife and tied it around Beech's midsection so that he carried it in the small of his back where it wouldn't easily be found.

"Now will you go to sleep?" McClintock said.

"If you're sure we won't have any more callers." He shifted around on the straw, trying to get comfortable.

The rattle of the key in the lock woke them; it was almost dawn and a thin grayness was beginning to melt away the night. They were taken outside. Jacob Spaniard was there, and Stark, and three armed Mexican guards.

"Time to go now," Spaniard said.

"I thought you woke us for tea," McClintock said.

"You still make jokes," Spaniard said. One of the Mexicans held a lantern high and the light worked deep shadows into his face and made his gray hair seem almost white. "By tonight you will not be thinking of anything funny to say." He pointed to the mountains. "Stark will take you to the base. From there—well, you can go where you please. When the sun is high, the *banditos* will ride. I'll give them until nightfall, McClintock; they'll take no longer than that to find you."

"What's going to keep Stark from shooting us in the back?" Will Beech asked.

"He'll be unarmed," Spaniard said. "Besides, Stark does not want to go into the mountains alone."

"Let me ask you something," McClintock said. "You came to Mexico with two men, Cash Randolph and a halfwit named Mushy. What happened to them?"

"The *banditos* killed them. I managed to escape. Somehow that impressed Calaveras. The next time we met, we became friends." He took out three cigars and gave one to Beech and McClintock. "Let's not have any hard feelings about this, shall we? I'm a man protecting what's mine. We're all relentless, ruthless men, are we not? I have my direction and you have yours, McClintock. And you, Beech, you have a certain relentlessness too. Yes you have. It's the pursuit of yourself, and your own courage. Why else did you brace Stark? But we've wasted enough time. I'm sorry you'll get no horses. Man is destined to make his last journey afoot."

He turned then and walked back to the huge house and Stark's horse was brought up and he stepped to the saddle, motioning for them to move out.

• • •

Finley Burkhauser was at the Army post, Fort Sam Houston, having his wound checked and dressed by the contract surgeon when the telegram finally found him; he read it and swore for a full minute without repeating himself although he had to use English, Spanish, some Kiowa and Comanche to do it. The surgeon was surprised and the two orderlies impressed, then Burkhauser rushed out to inquire about the loan of a fast horse to the nearest railroad station.

The post adjutant supplied a rangy buckskin and Burkhauser left for San Antonio, fuming because two and half days had been wasted in chasing him down. At the depot he left the horse with the station agent with instructions to turn it over to the sergeant who would call for it later, bought his ticket to Laredo and got on the train when it arrived forty-one minutes late.

Trains, in Burkhauser's opinion, were a pox on the landscape, always going too fast and layering everything along the right of way with cinders and coal smoke. Now he felt that the fireman was laying down on the job and the engineer was too timid to press the throttle valve to the open position; by his watch they were only averaging thirty-one miles an hour, a ridiculous speed to travel when a man was in a hurry.

He was the first down from the coach when it pulled into the station at Laredo, and Lieutenant

Braden and Captain Fuller met him; they had a rig waiting and although Burkhauser protested, Fuller took him to Fort McIntosh, a few miles north of town. This waste of time put Burkhauser in a lock-jawed fury and ushering him into Fuller's office didn't soothe him any.

Fuller sat down behind his desk and Braden leaned against the wall. Fuller pointed his finger at Finley Burkhauser and said, "Let's get one thing straight: we don't trade the life of one Texas Ranger for another one. You're not crossing the river."

"How the hell are you goin' to stop me?"

Fuller sighed and nodded and Braden opened the door; three Rangers stepped in and waited. Fuller said, "Lock him in the stockade." He switched his glance to Burkhauser. "Now if you want to put up a fight, I can guarantee you right now that Holliday, Anderson, and Willis can lick you. But you're goin', walking upright like a man with a little sense, or horizontal. Make up your mind right now."

Burkhauser turned his head slowly and looked at the three men; he knew them well, and he knew that Fuller wasn't making a cheap brag. He blew out a breath and nodded. "Let's walk." He turned to the door, then stopped and looked at Fuller. "You really figured it'd take three to put me down?"

"At least, and that's only because you've got a bum arm."

"Well," Burkhauser said, "that makes me feel some better. How long are you goin' to keep me locked up?"

"I don't know. Until we hear from McClintock or Spaniard. I just don't know, Finley. They got that railroad detective too."

"Beech?"

"Yes, that's his name. Too bad." He waved his hand. "Go on and behave yourself."

"Now let's not ask too much, Captain," Braden said, smiling.

"The point's duly noted," George Fuller said and cleared out his office by waving his arm violently a few times.

The flanks of the mountains were bathed in the clean morning sun. Stark stopped and turned in the saddle and the Mexican guards lowered their rifles. He pointed to a slash that climbed to the first ridge. "Game trails there. Take your pick." He crossed his hands on the saddle horn and smiled thinly. "I'll tell you something, McClintock. I begged Mr. Spaniard to put a gun in your hand. Did you ever want something so bad you could taste it? I wanted you two, one at a time or together. I wanted to shoot you in the guts."

"Try and live with your disappointment," McClintock suggested. "Will, you got any partin' advice for the *pistolero*?"

"What do I want to waste my time for?" Beech said.

The planes of Stark's face were hard and he stared at them a moment, then wheeled his horse and rode back toward the hacienda, a good two miles away. McClintock stood there, watching them until they began to grow small in the distance, then he turned and looked at the flank of the mountain.

"We'd travel faster in the valley, but we wouldn't last out the day. The *banditos* could see us from up there and run us down. Our only chance is in the hills."

"And not much of a chance," Beech said.

"No, not much, but still a chance. We can't make any mistakes at all. You understand?"

McClintock sat down and took off his boots and told Beech to get rid of his shoes. "Too easy to track," he said. He took his knife and took his coat apart at the seams and fashioned wraparounds, using his belt, cut into long thongs, to tie the footgear. He would permit nothing to be wasted. The remaining cloth was folded and wrapped around his waist and the boot tops made two knife sheaths. Belt buckle, buttons, and left over pieces of thong went into his pockets.

He was then ready to start climbing, after using an hour of precious time. Cutting a bushy twig, he made Beech go first and followed along, brushing out their tracks. He kept telling Beech to step on the rocks, the hard patches of ground and soon Beech was leaving no trail at all and McClintock threw away the branch.

Then he took the lead, working higher and staying to ground that gave him the best cover. He did not try to put a great deal of distance between the valley floor and where they were; rather he selected a route that would be difficult to follow on horseback, and one that left no sign.

There was no talk, no explanations; McClintock did a thing and his reasons were his own. He kept working toward a portion of the mountain laced by gullies and finally he found what he wanted, a trail well used, and a nest in the rocks where shrubs and saplings abounded.

This was a good hiding place, shielded on all sides, and McClintock immediately began to work. He selected a round rock the size of his fist, and a powerful sapling that could be bent into a bow. He measured the swing of this several times, then cut the branches where the sapling forked and stoutly bound the rock in place. Several times he drew the sapling back and let it fly until he was satisfied that it would do the job, then he had Will Beech do it, bending it just right so that it arced out toward a target as high as a horseman's head.

Then McClintock tied it back, in an exact position and hunkered down. The sun was starting down. He said, "Four hours to dark. This trail's pretty well used."

"We wait here?"

He nodded. "The more we move, the more liable we are to be seen." He looked up at the flat top of a big boulder overlooking the trail. "Come dark I'll belly flat on that." He picked up a small pebble. "When you hear this roll off, cut the thong. I'll stand by with the knife in case something goes wrong."

"Suppose there's more than one—"

"We'll let 'em go on by. I'm after horses and guns. Or one horse and one gun. We'll take this a piece at a time, partner." His smile reassured Will Beech. "I figure a man ain't done in until they bury him, and I don't get the feelin' that my face is bein' patted with a shovel."

"With horses we could make for the border."

"A man would think that. But we'd never make it. Too much Mexico between here and too many *banditos*. And no one to help us, *amigo*. Every hand against us. They're all afraid of the *banditos*."

"Then what do we do?"

"Ain't figured that out yet. But I will, when the time comes." He put his fingers to his lips. "Rest. Come dark we've both got to be wide-eyed and bushy-tailed. If you want to live, partner, you talk in whispers and walk like a shadow and leave no sign. You got to go, then you dig a hole and cover it like a cat. Understand?"

"Anything you say, Jim. It goes with me."

"Then let's learn how to wait."

SIX

To wait was to be silent and motionless. Waiting was thinking and Jim McClintock wondered if he should have explained to Will Beech the things that had been obvious to him. He was certain that the *banditos* would search this part of the mountains first; it was closer to Spaniard's ranch where the game would be set free. He also felt sure that they were in no danger of being shot if they were spotted for the *banditos* had to take them alive and kicking or there'd be no sport to it at all.

It all added up to a fighting chance in McClintock's mind. That he stood with small odds of winning was a foregone conclusion, but he figured to claw the *banditos* up a bit before they were captured.

In the late afternoon when the sun seemed hottest, they heard horsemen on the higher trails and they crouched in hiding as they worked down and passed their place; he judged twenty-five or thirty, by the sounds of their passing.

When the sounds faded and the dust settled, they looked at each other and endured their thirst and went on waiting. Dusk came, and night with a clear sky and a pat of butter moon. McClintock climbed onto the still warm rock and carried his knife in his hand. He waited there, measuring time by feeling the rock cool.

There was no wind at all, not even a breath of it and the only sounds were made by mice and other small game going about their nightlong hunt for food. McClintock's thirst was beginning to bother him and his empty stomach kept growling softly and he forced himself to be motionless, forced himself to wait. Then he heard them coming back, a large group strung out along the narrow trail; they came past his hiding place in single file, laughing and talking and he let them pass on. The dust swirled thick about him but he had counted them this time, nineteen, not all of them; there would be some stragglers.

He had a five minute wait although it seemed like an hour, then three more came through and he was torn with the urge to jump them, but one of them turned in the saddle and yelled, to someone still down the dark back trail and McClintock let himself go easy.

There was one more.

The three *banditos* rode on and their dust was still atingle in his nose when two more came along the trail. McClintock had only wanted one, but he had no choice now. He gauged the moment, kicked some loose pebbles down and Beech's knife let go the bent sapling. It whistled around and the rock struck the last *bandito* at the base of the skull, sounding like a large honeydew melon accidentally dropped on hard ground.

The first man sawed his horse to a stop and turned at the sound and McClintock jumped off the rock, landing on him squarely, knife driving down and deep; they fell together and then McClintock slowly got up, pulling his knife free.

At the smell of blood, one horse bolted; the other stood trembling and shy. Beech came from his hiding place and they quickly stripped the two men of everything, clothing, weapons, ammunition, and canteens; there were two, one partially filled, the other full.

McClintock flogged the standing horse with his hat, driving it on down the trail. Beech opened his mouth to speak, but McClintock said, "We're better off afoot. Let's go."

They gathered up everything and started climbing in the rocks, going high, climbing for better than an hour. Then McClintock found a pocket that looked good and stopped; he squatted on the ground and uncorked the partially full canteen, offering it to Will Beech first.

They drank in turns, sips at a time until the heavy thirst left them. Somewhere away from them, a gun bounced echoes three times.

Jim McClintock said, "The horses came back. They won't get much sleep tonight." He looked at Beech and smiled. "They'll do a lot of cussin' and thrashin' around and they'll worry more about what they'll tell Calaveras than they will about findin' us." He got up and moved about the cramped crevice they used as a hiding place. At first glance it seemed to be a fissure, a splitting of a huge boulder, when it really opened up into a sandy pit sheltered by a huge rock overhang. They could crawl back at least twenty yards and McClintock supposed that even a fire would go undetected, but he wasn't fool enough to find out.

They changed clothes, then took inventory. Beech had come into a .44-40 Winchester and ninety rounds of ammunition, and some matches, two guitar strings, a poor quality knife with folding blade, the canteen, and a small leather bag containing dried meat and some corn. McClintock inherited a .45-90 Sharps carbine and fifty rounds of ammunition, a full canteen, a bag containing meat, and a heavy blanket which had fallen off when the horse bolted. He also found tobacco and papers.

Their old clothes were carefully buried, then McClintock rolled a smoke and enjoyed it. Beech said, "It's hard for me to accept, losing the horses." He shook his head. "I just can't get it out of my mind that we could have got out of here with the horses."

"It's the kind of a mistake the *banditos* expect us to make," McClintock said softly. "I know it's hard to get through your head, Will, but there's just no place for us to go. We wouldn't make the border. No, our best bet is to foot it in the hills like Indians. We can make it damned tough on the *banditos*. And who knows what kind of luck we'll have?" He reached out and slapped Beech on the leg. "Let's get out of here."

"The *banditos* will be swarming all over these hills," Beech warned.

"Sure, but if they're up there movin' around, we'll be able to see what's goin' on and be where they ain't."

They climbed out of the fissure and paused to listen and to look around. Below them, on the trail, horsemen moved carefully; the flavor of dust drifted up to them and McClintock nudged Beech and they worked their way even higher.

By climbing where horsemen could not go, they were able to move clean to the ridge, and it was almost dawn when they made it. Although the night was cold, they were perspiring from the climb; they bellied down in a jumble of rocks along the ridge and drank water and ate some of the meat.

Beech said, "Jim, give me a straight answer: How long can we last?"

McClintock considered this carefully. "Well, I guess it's all how you think of lastin'. I guess you mean, when can I get back to my own place, doin' my own things like I always did? For that, I have no answer."

"I'm beginning to understand you, Jim, and I

can't say how I feel, angry or what. But it's very plain to me now why you weren't interested in the horses. I envy you. I wish I could accept the thought of dying so calmly."

"Who the hell says I'm calm about it?" McClintock asked. "Will, I knew I wasn't goin' to get out of this when Spaniard had us locked up. So instead of worryin' about all the things I'm goin' to miss by not goin' back, I just work on how much it's goin' to cost Calaveras and Spaniard to take me apart joint by joint and build a fire on my bare belly. What the hell is there to dyin' anyway? It's just an event, like birth. What goes on in between is what counts, Will."

Beech said, "I might as well be frank with you, Jim. I envy you. Your courage, the way you are. Somehow—and I just don't know how—I've got to learn to be that way."

"What for, Will?"

"So that I won't be sorry when it comes time to die."

Jacob Spaniard had a glass of wine at seven o'clock, then went to his library; it was his habit to read an hour before dinner for the combination of good wine and a good book stimulated his appetite. There was, he thought, no substitute for being rich. As a child he had lived in luxury, grown up in it, and during the Rebellion he had enjoyed the privileges of a rich man's son:

exemption from military service—he had purchased the services of two stupid Irishmen to take his place—and an important post in supply department, which allowed him to maintain the façade of doing a duty to his country.

Spaniard stood to inherit his father's business, but a year after the war there was no business, no money, no nothing. He was broke, completely broke, and he had a wife and two children to support; this was nearly impossible for a man without a singular skill.

From friends he borrowed barely enough to take him west, a move he hated, but there was no choice for he simply could not accept this position of poverty, could not have people look at him and see him and remember what he once was.

Spaniard found Texas no different than Indiana, except that nearly everyone was poor; it was a status he could not adjust to, although his wife did, and the children; resilient children, didn't mind at all.

He found so many people to dislike, so many to hate. He hated the bartender because he made nine dollars a week regularly and he hated the cattlemen and the merchants and that damned shoemaker, that stupid German with his broken English and funny mustache who charged him eighty cents to fix his boots.

A servant announced dinner and Jacob Spaniard put his book aside and went through the huge hall to the dining room. Tapestry hung on the walls soaked up the candlelight; it shined on the long table heavy with silver and good glass. He took his place at the head of the table and spoke to a servant who hovered near the sideboard. "Have you called my wife and daughter?"

"*Sí, jefe.*"

"Tell them to come down now or I'll have them brought down."

"*Sí.*" The servant scurried out and Spaniard sat down and adjusted the napkin to his throat. A moment later the servant came back, then May Spaniard and her mother came to the table and sat down. Spaniard looked at his wife, small, thin-boned, and silent.

He studied her a moment, then said, "Martha, have you nothing to say to me at all?"

It seemed that she was not going to answer him, then she raised her head and looked at him. "What do you want me to say? Those two men may be dying tonight and you expect me to sit here and eat?"

Jacob Spaniard pointed to the empty place. "Harry's plate is upside down. Cry for him."

"I can't," she said. "No more than I can cry for you. Please excuse me."

"No," he said. "Martha, you've fought me for years. I won't have it, do you understand? A man can stand just so much."

"Yes, I suppose that's true. But what is it you've

had to stand that's so terrible, Jacob? Blisters on your hands? Sweat on your face? Was it all such a terrible disgrace?" She got up slowly. "I'm going to my room now. I'm going to lock the door. Goodbye, Jacob."

"Goodbye?" He frowned. "What do you mean? Martha, sit down!"

Slowly she shook her head. "No more. Why don't you send me to the hills?" She stared at him a moment, then turned and walked out of the room. He raised his hand as though to signal the servants to stop her, then he let his hand fall slowly.

"Do you know what she meant, May?"

"Yes," she said and began to serve herself.

He studied her at length. "You're against me too."

"No, not really against you, Father. I just can't be for the things you're for. Somehow I just can't make friends with darkness."

"You talk like your mother."

"But I'm not like her," May said evenly. "Father, before you put Jim McClintock and Will Beech into the hills, I slipped them each a knife." She studied his expression and laughed. "I'd have given them guns if they hadn't been all locked up. But a knife to Jim McClintock—"

He reared to his feet, upsetting his chair, and dashed to the door, yelling, "Stark! Stark, where are you!" He grabbed a servant loitering in the hall. "Get Stark! *Andale*!" Then he came back and righted his chair and sat down, his face heavy with concern.

May's smile remained sweet and simple. "What are you thinking of, Father? Of the kind of man Jim McClintock is? Men may be dying in the mountains tonight, Father, but I rather think it is someone besides Jim McClintock."

"Shut up and let me think!"

"What do you want to think of? Of what Calaveras will think? You're supposed to send him harmless, desperate toys, Father. But now you've sent him a tiger with sharp claws."

Stark came into the room. "You wanted me—"

"You damned idiot! McClintock and Beech had knives!" He waved his hand at his daughter. "She slipped them to them."

Stark's eyes touched her, cold and expressionless. "How was I to know, Mr. Spaniard? Hell, you can't expect me to know everything." He fell into a brief, reflective silence. "Calaveras is liable to lose a few men before he has his fun. What the hell, he can't have everything his way."

"How would you like to ride into the mountains and explain that to him?" Spaniard asked. He scraped a hand across his mouth and sat with his lips mashed against his knuckles. "That damned McClintock is an Indian. Beech— I don't count him for much—but that McClintock knows how to fight." He looked at

141

Stark. "I want you to get a message to Calaveras."

"You want me to signal him in the morning from the tower?"

"I want you to get on your damned horse and go to his camp," Spaniard said. "You can make it by noon tomorrow if you leave now. Get your horse and some provisions. I'll write a letter that you can give him; it'll explain—"

"Just what will it explain?" May asked. "Your innocence, Father?"

"I told you to shut up. Go to your room and stay there." He turned his attention to Stark. "Go on now and don't waste time."

Nodding, Stark turned to the door and stopped there. "What about her, Mr. Spaniard? How long are you goin' to put up—"

"It's my affair and I'll handle it."

"Just as you say," Stark murmured and left the room. Spaniard pushed his dinner aside and lit a cigar.

"No appetite, Father?"

"I told you to get out of here."

"Why don't you have the servants drag me to my room?"

"Don't be ridiculous," Spaniard said.

"You're right. It's a time to be honest, isn't it? You've always believed that Calaveras has his camp in the mountains because you've given him permission. That was a very comforting thing to believe, but the truth of it is that he's there because he wanted to be and he'd be there whether you liked it or not. You're really not anything, Father. I don't think you ever have been, and perhaps that's why it was so impossible to live with yourself when you had nothing, because you always thought of yourself as a king when really you weren't good enough to be a king's servant."

He managed to reach her with his slap and knocked her out of her chair to the floor. She calmly pushed her dress down over her slim calves and got up, her cheek livid.

"I didn't know you could be so kind," she said and left the room.

Visibility from the ridge was excellent; the day was cloudless and hot and from the valley shimmers of heat rose to distort McClintock's view. Will Beech slept; they would do this in shifts from now on, one sleeping and one watching. Three times McClintock had seen movement below on the trails and the *banditos* were thick in the small valley on the other side. They searched it carefully, figuring that McClintock and Beech had driven deeper in search of water and a hiding place.

It was, McClintock decided, a trick they would soon catch onto; by nightfall they would be back on this side of the valley, combing the mountain like a boy searching out fleas on his dog.

He saw the rider approaching the pass and woke Beech, who grunted and rubbed his eyes.

"Too far away to tell who it is," he said.

"Stark," McClintock said. "See how now and then the sun catches the silver on his saddle?" He picked up his rifle. "Let's go."

"Go where?"

"The head of the pass," McClintock said. "He's comin' the same way we did, so it must be the only trail into these mountains for miles."

"In broad daylight?"

"You look like a *bandito*," McClintock said and started down.

Will Beech looked at him and suddenly grinned. His face was dirty and dark with whiskers and the sun had been working on him, darkening him even further. "Yeah?" he said. "I feel just like I'd finished the tenth lesson in a mail order course on how to be scared."

"Hell, I got my diploma years ago," McClintock admitted and kept on moving.

He took a route that he figured would bisect the trail; they slid and jumped, made no attempt at all to keep out of sight. Then McClintock stopped, standing spraddle-legged on a large boulder. He put two fingers in his mouth and whistled and almost laughed when Stark, farther down the trail, jerked his head up in surprise. He waved at the rider then jumped down and disappeared from Stark's view.

"It figures that the *banditos* know Stark by sight and it figures that Stark knows the location of the *bandito* camp." He grinned and winked. "Catch on?"

"No," Beech said.

They hid along the trail, where it narrowed sharply and Stark rode right past them, suspecting nothing. Then McClintock said, "Freeze or I'll blow out your spine."

Stark halted his horse with his knees and slowly started to raise his hands and stopped when Beech said, "Don't do that!" He moved out and took Stark's pearl-handled pistols and held them with his finger through the trigger guards. He lifted Stark's carbine from the boot, ejected the contents of the magazine and put the cartridges in his own belt. He booted the empty rifle and unloaded the pistols.

Stark said, "Why don't you come around where I can see you, McClintock."

"I don't want to see you. Put his cartridges in his shell belt, Will." Then he walked around and stood in front of Stark. "Give him back his pistols, Will." He waited and Stark sat loosely in the saddle. "I don't suppose you'd care to say what you're doin' in the mountains, huh?" He grinned. "Well, I can guess. You're carryin' a message to Calaveras. Search him, Will."

It took only a moment to find the note; Beech read it and said, "Good guess, Jim."

"Guess, hell, it was the only answer. All right, Stark, you lead the way to Calaveras. We'll walk along behind you and if you think you can jump and run, figure that this .45-90 has one hell of a long reach."

"McClintock, I've got to give it to you; you've got more brass than a fireman's band. Hell, I've got a pass in and out of Calaveras's camp and even I don't like the idea of going there."

"Tell you how it is, *pistolero*. Runnin' around these hills, killin' a *bandito* or two is just doin' a lot of choppin' and makin' no chips fly. Now you got to ask yourself just what we got to lose? We'd never make it to the border. If the *banditos* didn't get us, Spaniard would put a hundred riders in the saddle, and offer fifty *pesos* to any peon who pointed at us and yelled *gringo*. So what the hell, we ought to raise a little Cain, huh? Maybe kill ourselves some fancy dressin' *pistolero*, huh?" He looked at Stark and smiled and his eyes were like chips of pond ice. "I guess you can measure what's left of your life up to the moment you make your first mistake, huh?"

The gunman looked at Will Beech, then back to Jim McClintock. "I had a feelin' of death the first minute I saw you, Ranger. It was a smell. Mr. Spaniard has it."

"And you have it," McClintock said softly. "All right, Stark, let's go."

· · ·

Captain Fuller had to admit that Finley Burkhauser was probably the best-mannered prisoner he had ever had in the stockade; he gave the guards no trouble at all and daily swept out his cell and tidied the place generally. In the evenings he played cards with the guards by thrusting his hands through the bars of his cell door.

By the third evening the word was getting around that Burkhauser's touch at poker was lost; he had already dropped thirty dollars and the games began to turn out five handed. Dealing through the bars became an inconvenience so the guard opened the cell door and the game continued.

At eleven o'clock, Burkhauser had lost another thirty dollars; he had the deal, a new, slick deck, and quite accidentally dropped several cards on the floor. He bent to pick them up and when he straightened he had Elmer Fanning's pistol in his hand.

They sat there, looking stupid and he relieved them of their guns. "Let's all be nice and quiet now," Burkhauser suggested.

Fanning said, "You wouldn't shoot us, would you?"

"No, but I'd put a nice dent in your skull. You like that idea?"

None of them did, so he put them in the cell,

locked the door and put the key in his pocket. He explained the situation. "If you start yellin' your heads off, chances are that I won't make it off the post. But someone's going to get some lumps on the head and they'll be mad at you as well as the captain. So why don't you gents sit nice and quiet for five minutes? You can give a man that much of a chance, can't you?"

They looked at each other and Fanning nodded. He unbuckled his shell belt and handed it through the bars. "I'd hate to see you go south with five beans in the wheel," he said. "You know my horse. The saddle's in the barn, rifle, blankets, everything."

"I hope you fellas can lie your way out of this," Burkhauser said, and buckled on the shell belt before leaving.

Captain Fuller was checking some reports before signing them and the commotion from the guardhouse drew his attention, then irritated him and he got up and walked across the parade ground to see what the devil was going on. A crowd had already gathered and he bulled his way through.

He sized up the whole thing at a glance then took off his hat and threw it on the floor. "I suppose someone is going to tell me he's already left the post."

The guard at the main gate cleared his throat. "I recognized Fanning's buckskin and I thought—

well dammit, Captain, it was a natural mistake, dark and all!"

"Someone open this cell door and let these guardians of law and order out," Fuller said.

"He took the key, sir," Fanning said.

"By God, now that's just dandy. Well, I've always wanted to lock a man up and throw away the key." He looked at the men in the cell and shook his head sadly. "In the morning, if the blacksmith isn't busy, I'll have him come around and see what he can do about getting the door open. If he's busy, we'll just have to wait another day, won't we?" He turned and clumped out, his boot heels striking hard on the porch.

"Aw, hell," Elmer Fanning said and flopped down on the bunk. "Anyway, I hope he makes it across." He raised up on an elbow and stared at the men crowded into the cell block. "All right, what the hell are you lookin' at? Ain't you seen a man in jail before?"

Finley Burkhauser swam the horse across the river, by passing the regular crossing because there were always two Rangers on duty there and he'd already put a gun on four and it left a bad taste in his mouth. Fuller, he imagined, was on one of his rampages and Fanning would have to take most of it and this bothered Burkhauser because Elmer was a good man

149

and would have made corporal in another year. Now he might not ever make it.

On the Mexican side, Burkhauser paused to pour water from his boots and wring his pants dry, then he stepped into the saddle, skirted the Mexican village and rode in a southwesterly direction. The country was not unfamiliar to him because he had been through it several times before, chasing white renegades or *banditos* from Calaveras's bunch.

He was, in a general sense, familiar with the location of Spaniard's rancho although he had never been there; he had heard of it from the Mexican army and the *rurales* who did not go there unless specifically ordered to do so. That Calaveras used the mountains as his hideout headquarters was knowledge possessed by every peon from Santa Rose to Saltillo and they always crossed themselves when they spoke his name.

Toward morning he rested briefly, no more than two hours, then moved on, making every attempt to stay in the open and be seen. He wore out that day and camped the night on what he thought was Jacob Spaniard's land. He built a fire and made some coffee and laid down his blankets and even slept for a time, thinking that he had miscalculated a bit, but then the hard bung of a rifle muzzle against his ribs told him that he had not. An accented voice said, "Wake carefully, señor, or you will never wake at all."

He opened his eyes first; they ringed him, all heavily armed, their eyes like melted chocolate, and as expressionless. Burkhauser was relieved of his weapons, then allowed to sit up.

"It was very foolish for you to build a fire, señor. I am Sanchez, *segundo* for Señor Spaniard. You will mount your horse, *por favor*?"

When they were mounted and the fire was put out, they turned southwest again and rode out the night. In the first faint flush of dawn, Burkhauser could make out the rancho, the walls looming gray and forbidding like some desert stronghold. Sentries atop the palisade signaled and the gates were opened as they approached and after they passed through they were closed and barred.

Burkhauser was impressed with the immensity of the place; he was taken to the main house and Jacob Spaniard came out and stood on the edge of the porch where the strong morning sun struck him fully. He looked at Burkhauser for a minute, then said, "Knock him off his horse."

There was no time to look around; Burkhauser rather sensed the direction of the blow and slipped off to one side, Indian style, and the Mexican who had swung his rifle lost his balance and fell heavily. This frightened the horses and they backed and milled and Burkhauser stepped toward the porch.

Instantly a half dozen rifles were pointed at

him and he looked at Jacob Spaniard and said, "You can't be as scared as all that."

Spaniard scowled, then waved his hands and Sanchez and his men walked away; they stopped under a grove of trees a good fifty yards from the porch and waited there.

"You carry your arm stiffly," Spaniard said. "Is that where my son put his bullet?"

Burkhauser nodded. "You should have seen where a Ranger put *his* bullet. Your boy was pretty stupid, Jake. Takes after his father, I suppose." He turned his head slowly and looked around. "Where's McClintock and Beech?" He looked back at Spaniard. "Dead?"

"No, not to my knowledge." He laughed softly. "That McClintock never does what he's supposed to do, does he? I turned him and Beech loose in the hills for the *banditos* to play with. But my daughter had slipped them a couple of knives."

"Well," Burkhauser said, "I guess they ain't dead at that. Someone ought to have told you about Jim; he's pretty tricky. When he was ten he got took by the Kiowas and it was a little over a year before he escaped. He put in four years with the cavalry durin' the Comanche trouble. Was I to sum it up for you I'd say that Jim knows how to handle himself."

"Beech will slow him down," Spaniard said. "The man's a coward."

"Well now, just what's a coward, Jake?"

The door behind Spaniard opened and May stepped onto the porch. She said, "I'm sorry to see you here, Mr. Burkhauser. You should know my father well enough not to trust him or believe him."

"Go back in the house," Spaniard advised. "Go sit with your mother, May. Read to her or something." May remained where she was. Spaniard turned his attention back to Finley Burkhauser, then he lifted his hand and pointed to an adobe enclosure behind the stables, in the far corner of the compound. "That's going to be your home for the next ten years. I had it built special and it never had an occupant. Since you've taken prisoners to Huntsville, you'll recognize it as one of the cell blocks and exercise yards."

"It's funny the way some men get pleasure," Burkhauser said.

"It isn't pleasure," May said evenly. "You might even say it's pain, all the times he's not had his way, or what he wanted, or all the things he's felt that he's deserved and been denied." She looked at her father. "Aren't you going to hit me again?"

He reached out and pushed her back a step, but that was all. Raising his hand brought the guards back. "Put him in the cell," Spaniard said. "I'll look in on him later. And beat him before he's fed." He saw the expression in

Burkhauser's eyes and pointed his finger like a gun. "You want to fight, huh? Go ahead. It won't get you anything except a cracked skull."

"Why don't you come down here and do the job?" Burkhauser asked.

"Because I pay to have it done. I'm not afraid of you, Finley. Don't think that for a minute."

Sanchez prodded him with the rifle. "Move, señor. Or shall you be carried?"

"I guess I'll walk," Burkhauser said and was marched across the compound. The cell was adobe, small, with a very high window. He was put inside and the door was closed and locked. The straw on the floor had been brought in from the stable yard, clotted with mud and manure.

Sanchez spoke through the small window in the door. "I do not understand what it is you have done to Señor Spaniard to make him so full of revenge."

"I locked him in a place like this for ten years," Burkhauser said. "He killed a shoe-maker." This made no impression on Sanchez, who considered life fairly cheap at best. "You don't think that's right, huh? Locking up a man just because he shoots another."

Sanchez's shoulders rose and fell. "It is hard to say, for I have killed men. No one locked me in a cell. The shoemaker must have offended Señor Spaniard's honor."

"You think he's got any?" Burkhauser asked.

Sanchez did not answer because someone approached the door and it was unlocked. Pete Tanner and Harry Scanlon stepped in, wrinkling their noses at the strong odor of ammonia.

"Nice place you got here," Tanner said. "I guess you remember me, huh?"

"Now how could I forget you?"

Tanner laughed. "We're goin' to give you your lumps. And you might as well know that I'll enjoy it."

"You figure on talkin' a bruise on me?" Burkhauser asked.

It dug into Tanner and he lunged forward and was kicked in the groin. Tanner folded like an old blanket and then Scanlon rushed in, pinning Burkhauser against the cell wall, hurting his bad arm, yelling for Sanchez to come in and help him.

It took Sanchez and another guard to hold Burkhauser while Scanlon did his work like a man chopping down a stubborn tree. He was sweating when he was finished and they left Burkhauser unconscious on the floor when they stepped out and locked the door.

SEVEN

Major Alfred Murdo was by nature a sound sleeper and the Officer of the Day knocked several times, loudly, before he got a response. Murdo sat up and put a match to the lamp on his side table as the OD came in. "Sorry to disturb you, sir, but march orders just came through. Direct from Washington."

Murdo took the wire and squinted a bit before putting on his glasses. He read it several times, then stood up and scratched his stomach. "It seems that Captain Fuller has more political pull than I gave him credit for." He reached for the cigar butt in the ashtray and bent slightly forward as the OD offered the light. Murdo was a man in his late fifties, a thin, wasted shell of a man who had never known a day of sickness. "You've alerted the company commanders?"

"Yes, sir. They'll be ready to load the train as soon as it reaches the siding, sir. Approximately two hours. We should be at Fort McIntosh at dawn, sir."

Murdo puffed on his cigar and dressed quickly. "Damned if I know how he did it. I've been wanting to take a command across the border for three years now." He looked at the OD and smiled. "A month's pay says we bag this bandit, Fleming." He let a laugh bubble from the cavity of his chest. "You know what this means? We wouldn't be crossing the river without the blessing of the Mexican government. That means we'll be joined by the Mexican army."

"Frankly, sir, that fails to excite me. I just can't count on any of them for much support."

"We can at least figure that they'll stay out of our way," Murdo said. "I want to see the company commanders in headquarters in a half hour."

"Yes, sir." The OD saluted and hurried out and Murdo tugged on his boots, took a few final drags on his cigar, then left his quarters. The night was brisk and clear and the post was quiet except for C, D, and F Companies; their barracks were bright with light and there was activity at the stable and farrier yard.

The orderly, warned that the major would arrive, had the lamps lighted and a fire going in the pot-bellied stove when Murdo stepped into the outer office. At his desk he lit a fresh cigar, put up some roll maps and studied them for a time, then the first of his commanders arrived, early, as he expected they would.

They took chairs, a captain and two first lieutenants, all serious men with a lot of serious duty behind them. "Gentlemen, Captain Fuller of the Texas Rangers has somehow managed— through the governor, I suppose—to wrangle official approval of a punitive expedition into Mexico in pursuit of Calaveras, the bandit." He picked up a pointer and began making sweeping moves across the map. "I don't suppose there's a private on the post who doesn't know that Calaveras has a headquarters somewhere in the mountains past the Rio Salado. That's privately owned land and under the protection of the Mexican government. However, now that we have official permission to take an armed command into Mexico, we can cross that land with impunity."

"What can we expect from the Mexican army, sir?" the captain asked.

Murdo thrust his hands into his pockets. "To be safe, we should count on nothing. The Mexican army is riddled with graft. I think we all are safe in assuming that Calaveras couldn't operate such a large band of outlaws without the authorities turning their heads. It's my opinion that the Mexican army will stand clear. If we succeed, they have little to worry about. If we fail, their shirt tails will be clean in future deals with Calaveras." He glanced at each of them. "However, it is not my intention to fail, gentlemen."

"Excuse me, sir," the captain said. "But it's got me curious as how this permission was granted, especially at this time. The bandits haven't been too active. By that I mean, the newspapers haven't been setting up a cry and I don't know of any outraged citizens who've been writing their congressman."

"I won't know the details until I've talked with Captain Fuller at Laredo," Murdo said. "However, I'll make a guess. It's my feeling that perhaps the Mexican government is not really aware of *our* purpose in entering Mexico. That is to say, I don't believe they understand that we want Calaveras. Knowing George Fuller, I'd say he's sold them a poke of beans. Yet it seems to me damned silly to waste this chance. After all, gentlemen, after we've brought Calaveras back to hang and broken up his band, we can make all sorts of suitable apologies to the Mexican government."

"Ah, politics," the captain sighed. "Truly an unusual way of life."

"Yes, and I'd sure like to know how Fuller did it. The governor is not an easy man to do business with." He waved his hand. "Dismissed. I'll inspect the command before loading."

Jim McClintock walked directly behind Stark's horse; there was no talk for McClintock was thinking and he knew that Stark was thinking too. He couldn't blame Stark; the man was measuring his chances, thinking them all out, and McClintock could follow the man's mind as easily as if he were able to get inside and rummage around.

Stark knew that he was valuable alive, and worth nothing dead. He was a prisoner yet he had a certain amount of control over McClintock and Beech because he knew where he was going and they didn't.

He could ride into Calaveras's camp unchallenged and they couldn't.

Stark took his time, thinking it all out, and he always came around in a circle to the fact that McClintock had to keep him alive. And it was this reasoning that forced him to make his move.

They were working through a long, timbered valley and Stark was crossing a stream, his horse splashing with each step. Timber grew close to the water on the other side; he had thirty yards to cover, and he'd reasoned it out, that McClintock wouldn't risk the noise of a shot, not really.

So he raked his horse with his spurs and jumped him forward and the horse started to lunge up the other bank when a hot rod struck him between the shoulder blades, sunk deep and hurting and the fire filled his chest while the strength ran out of him. Slowly he turned in the saddle and looked at McClintock, then started to fall; he would have fallen had not McClintock rushed forward and caught him. Beech grabbed the horse by the bridle and kept it from bolting and with a sudden movement, McClintock jerked out the knife he had thrown.

Stark died without uttering a word and

McClintock held him to the saddle. He spoke to Will Beech and nodded toward some saplings. "Cut a stout one with a wide fork."

Beech searched a moment, found one that suited McClintock, and cut it down. With pieces of Stark's rope, McClintock tied the butt of the sapling straight up, against Stark's back. He bent the branches in a bow and tied them under the horses's belly, then he fashioned a cross piece, lashed Stark to it and gave the horse a slap, sending him off.

McClintock cleaned the blade of his knife on grass and said, "We can't be far or he wouldn't have made his break. Figured I wouldn't risk a shot."

"I guess he was right about that," Beech said softly. "You think his horse will go on into Calaveras's—"

"Sure," McClintock said, gently interrupting. "We won't have any trouble followin' the tracks. I guess Stark will throw the camp in an uproar, comin' in dead and tied to the saddle. It may give us a chance to do somethin'."

"Like?"

McClintock shrugged. "Couldn't say. I'm a man who plays by ear."

Will Beech nodded, then said, "I couldn't have thrown that knife even if I knew how."

"You think not?"

"I know it." He fell silent a moment and

scratched himself; the clothes they had taken from the *banditos* were full of fleas with healthy appetites. "It's the way a man was raised, I guess. You've always done a thing that had to be done and worried about it afterward. Me, I've always hung back a little and waited for someone else to do it."

"And when someone didn't step up?"

"Then I'd do it," Beech said. "But liking it none."

"Who the hell likes it?" McClintock asked. "Tell you how it is, Will. I just never had time to stop and figure out what makes men like Stark not give a whoop about anythin' except what they want. Maybe they're just missin' somethin' in the head. But who cares? Do you care? I sure as hell don't. Never did and likely never will. The law's somethin' that's good for the people. It protects them against things they can't handle or understand. When I enforce the law, I don't stop and figure out how I can save some bum's life, and it don't interest me much if he gets another chance or not. All this is somethin' that men like Stark don't figure on and it usually does 'em in. They just can't get it through their head that we can get along without 'em." He looked around, then tucked his rifle in the crook of his arm. "Time to look into some horse tracks."

He entered the timber but stayed near the fringe of it and they walked nearly a mile before

Will Beech spoke. "Jim, if we get back to Jake Spaniard's place, have you got anything in mind?"

"If you got back, how would you get in short of haulin' up some artillery?"

"I was thinking of the girl," Beech said. "I don't claim to understand her, Jim? But I guess you do. I mean, why she sticks with him, the way he is." He walked on a way in silence. "Jim, you don't suppose Burkhauser would actually cross the border, do you?"

"Yes, he'll cross."

"But he must know—"

"He knows that too," McClintock said. "He just never learned how to give up, Will. None of us have: Spaniard, Finley, or me. Can't you see that we're alike?"

"Somehow it seems like a waste," Beech said. "You know what I mean. If Spaniard could only forget about—"

"He can't, so why even think about it."

"But the girl's different. That night in the cabin, you could tell that she wasn't—" He let it trail off. "There's good in her."

Jim McClintock stopped and turned to Will Beech. "What are you tryin' to talk yourself into anyway?" He looked at Beech, his eyes bloodshot, his cheeks lean and dirty and unshaven. "You goin' to follow me, gabbin' away like some pet parrot?"

Toward nightfall they left the valley to climb a flank of a steep rise; the valley had been narrowing to a bare fissure between two massive rocks and McClintock guessed that this was some high pass leading to meadow and water beyond.

It was dark when they made the ridge and looked down at the bright fires of Calaveras's camp. McClintock made a rough count and guessed that he had well over a hundred and fifty men. Add women and children and the total was closer to five hundred.

McClintock said, "Looks like one way in and one way out, but we'll make sure. From what I could see on the climb up, we're on the rim of a crater and an earthquake at one time or another must have opened up that pass."

"You want to scout the rim?" Beech asked.

"Had it in mind. Don't know of any other way of findin' out whether or not there's a trail up and over. My guess is that there ain't. But if we run into any guards tonight we can figure that there is."

They ate the last of their meat and corn and saved only a little water, then slowly, carefully made their way around the rim. They were in high country where the nights turned cold and around two o'clock the temperature had dropped to where they could make out their breath.

Dawn found them on the other side, near the

pass, hunkered down in the loose rock there; they had found no guards although McClintock saw a place which he thought was a passable climb for mounted men.

The sun was welcome and they stretched out and slept, letting the mounting heat of it soak them. Around noon they woke, bathed in sweat. They sipped water and McClintock studied the crater floor. It was huge, with water and good grass, then he drew Beech's attention to the pass.

Two cannon had been hauled in and were pointed at the pass. Powder and shot was stored nearby and three men were on duty at each gun.

"Now that's the most interestin' thing I've seen since Big Lulu lost her dress while in swimmin'."

"Who's Big Lulu?"

"Runs a sportin' house in Tascosa." He shook his head. "You wouldn't like her. Not your type at all. I put you down as a man who likes a woman a bit plump, sort of built for comfort, not for speed. Lulu's skinny as an ax handle, and just as hard."

"You sure know some interesting people," Beech admitted. "If we get out of this, how about taking me around?"

"Sure, what the hell?" He kept looking at the cannon. "You know, if a man had a couple of bags of that powder he could sure raise hell with that pass, couldn't he?" He stopped talking to watch a large body of horsemen ride through the pass; someone always seemed to be coming and going from the camp.

Beech said, "It gives you a funny feeling to be watching this and knowing they're looking for you."

"You ever watch a man search for somethin' he lost? He'll look under the bed and dresser and everywhere, then at last look in his pocket, where it was all the time. Same thing here. This is the last place they'll look for us."

"Do we have to be around here when they get around to it?"

McClintock grinned. "Damn it, you talk like that and I'll get to think you don't like it here." He rested his chin on his hands and studied the cannon. "The way I figure it, I'd put one bag to blow the pass closed, and another across where we found what looked like a trail. A couple of men could fort up there and hold off an army and if it got too hot, they could touch off some powder and bring one hell of a slide. It might buy the time we'd need to make some tracks."

"You just said a word that perks up my interest," Beech said.

"When it gets dark, I'll go down and see if I can steal some powder." Beech opened his mouth and McClintock shook his head. "This will take some Injun doin', and I've got experience. Besides, if I do somethin' stupid down there, there's no sense in us both payin' for it."

"I don't suppose you'd listen to a rebuttal to that, would you?"

"Nope," McClintock said.

"You're a hard man to argue with."

"Ain't it the truth though?"

Beech rolled over on his back and closed his eyes. "I know what a dog feels like laying in the sun. And I've got a strong wish to get back, find me a dog, and give him all my fleas." He opened his eyes and looked at Jim McClintock. "How come I'm beginning to talk about getting back?"

"You just put your mind on good whiskey and wild women for awhile and all hell couldn't stop you," McClintock advised. "I always did say that when you wanted a man to do somethin', don't waste his time by offerin' him somethin' good and proper. Make it a bottle or a woman and he'll charge hell with a teacup." He chuckled softly.

Governor E. Fillmore Stiles rode his private coach to Laredo, and was so determined to get there that he almost sided the Army train to get a clear right away. He was a large man, fat now, but still about him remained the suggestion of strength and great vigor. A coach took him directly to Fort McIntosh and George Fuller met him there. They went into Fuller's office and Stiles took a chair and the whiskey Fuller offered him. "When I got your wire, Governor, I was a bit surprised. That is to say, I didn't think you'd leave Austin."

"Why not?" Stiles asked. He clamped his lips together and his jowl quivered. "Just because a man grows fat behind a desk doesn't mean he can't get excited at the prospect of a fight." He leaned back and the oak in the chair protested, the joints creaking slightly. "I was nineteen the year I came to Texas; that was in 1846. We settled on a place near what is now Palestine; my father was a farmer and land owner from Tennessee, from an old family and he carried himself with honor. I mention this because it is important to grasp my family background, my frame of mind. At nineteen, Captain, I was a strong man, fully grown, and inclined to be arrogant. It pleased me to see a man take his hat off to me, or to step aside when I entered a room." He waved his hand. "I see your faint smile, sir, and I agree that it is justified. But to return to my purpose: Life was raw at best, and the weekly trip to the settlement was a break in a routine of hard work and little fun. It was at the settlement that I first saw Finley Burkhauser; he came into town on an Indian pony, dressed in leather, and bearing an enormous Kentucky rifle. I judged his age to be sixteen at the time, and later learned that I had only erred by a year. He was, I believe, the first Texas born I had ever seen; there was a wildness about him that was an instant challenge to me, and

I called him to the side of the street on the pretext of speaking to him and commanded him to remove his skin hat when he spoke to his betters."

Stiles shook his head and chuckled. "Well, sir, in plain view of men whose admiration and respect I courted, he got off his horse, put his rifle to one side, and proceeded to give me a thrashing. And as I recall, he never did take off his damned hat. Later, when some of my cuts had healed, I mentioned going to his camp; he was hunting and trapping somewhere along the Neeches. But wiser heads mentioned that Burkhauser might misconstrue the visit and shoot me before a full explanation of my presence was given." Stiles puffed gently on his cigar and accepted another whiskey. "That fall, I'd seen to it that a schoolhouse had been built and because there was no teacher, I took over this assignment. To my surprise, Burkhauser appeared at the door one day and asked if I could teach him to read and write. He was, to give him credit, an eager student, smart, and as determined a man as I've ever seen. Relentless would be the word to describe him; he attacked a thing with a single-mindedness that was worth watching. Come spring he was writing a clear hand and reading nearly as well as I. Of course, I'm saying that he did little else that winter save study."

He paused to rekindle his cigar and take a sip of whiskey. "For three years I heard nothing from him. I left Palestine and went to Austin to read law, and eventually practiced there for a time. Later I went to Abilene to serve as circuit judge. It was a raw country with damned little law and order and more often than not I was forced, by public pressure and threats of violence, to levy a fine where a long prison term would have been in order."

"I remember those days," Fuller said, smiling. "And I raised a little hell myself."

"High spirits never bothered me," Stiles said. "I recall vividly an instance where several cowboys got into a fight with pistols. One was killed and the wife of a merchant was killed. Feeling ran pretty high; the townspeople were pressing for a speedy trial and a hanging and the cattlemen were all for letting the two survivors go because no one was sure whose bullet actually killed the woman. The town was an armed camp with fighting on the street and stores being broken into and looted. The sheriff finally got a volunteer, a buffalo hunter, to sneak out of town and go for the Army at Fort Griffin. Two days later a cavalry detachment arrived, commanded by Lieutenant Finley Burkhauser. He cleaned up the town in short order without drawing a saber or pointing a carbine. However, a few heads on both sides bore lumps." He sat there and laughed at the memory. "Fuller, all my life I've been running into Burkhauser, and I'll be frank about it;

he's pulled me out of more than one tight spot. Now I have the chance to pay him back and I'll tell you straight out, I didn't mind a bit putting the pressure on a few congressmen and senators. In twenty years of politics you learn a lot about the men you deal with and some of the things you learn are better kept quiet. I merely prefaced my telegrams with the statement that I had been working on a book about men in public life in which I tell all." He spread his pudgy hands. "How could they refuse my simple request? I'll bet they were knocking on the President's door within the hour." He dropped his dead cigar in an ashtray. "Well, Mexico's been fending us off for years, claiming that the bandits are an internal problem that they are working hard to solve. It's a lie, but then politicians tell a lot of lies. But prior requests have always come through diplomatic channels; this time the President spoke to the Mexican Ambassador. That makes a big difference." He looked at George Fuller and raised an eyebrow. "Just as you reminded me of that small matter of an election irregularity that time in Uvalde County. Of course we both know there was nothing to it."

"Of course, Governor."

"But still it's something the public might not understand if they heard about it." He leaned slightly forward. "You weren't really going to grant an interview to the newspapers, were you?

Why, that whole thing blew over ten years ago."
He laughed and leaned back, relaxed now. "You
could scare a man with a wire like that, Fuller."

"Let's just say that it could stir a man, sir."

"Yes, a nice way to put it," Stiles said. He
slapped his knees and blew out his breath.
"Where's the damned Army?"

"Due to arrive. Major Murdo wired me earlier.
He has three companies of cavalry, a
quartermaster company, one of light artillery, and
a medical detachment."

Stiles's mouth dropped. "My God, is he
invading?" He took out a handkerchief and
wiped his palms. "Fuller, this is shaky business
anyway. Hell, I can excuse my part in this by
saying that I wanted the Texas border made safe
from the bandits but I never in God's name
thought for a minute that Murdo would actually
try to engage the bandits. This was to be a token
thrust, Fuller. A—a gesture while we recovered
Burkhauser and that other Ranger, whatever his
name is." He wiped his mouth with the handkerchief before putting it away. "Fuller, I've put
some old friends on the spot in Washington, if
this comes to an engagement between U.S. forces
and the Mexicans. I think we should reconsider
the whole thing, re-evaluate the whole situation.
Perhaps a company—"

Fuller interrupted him. "Governor, I don't think
that's a good idea at all. I've simply got to give

you this opportunity to be a hero to the State of Texas, even if it means putting your political future on the block, so to speak. Why, when these bandits are cleaned out and the people hear about it, they'll boot you back into office for another term in a landslide." He shrugged. "I suppose there will have to be a few explanations made to the Mexican government, but I'm sure Washington can convince them that our forces were attacked by the bandits and simply defended themselves. All along I felt pretty sure that you'd see it my way, sir. In fact, after I got your wire, I invited some newspaper people here. Thought you'd like to make a statement. Of course, if you don't want to, I can make a statement."

Stiles sat with his face solemn, his lips squashed together. "You're dangling an ax over my head, Fuller. I guess you know I'll have to do something about it when I get back to Austin."

"Well, Governor, you just go right ahead. You take my record and look it over good. You might even have others look it over but I'll tell you ahead of time what you'll find. Adherence to duty. Straight. Right down the line. No graft, no money in the pocket, no unaccountable bank deposits. You take a good look at the record, Governor, and if you can find one thing there to fire me for, I'll quit."

"Damn you, Fuller, you're the hardest kind of

man in the world to fight. Because you're honest."
He heaved his bulk out of the chair and took a
fresh cigar from his case; when he bent to
accept Fuller's light, he glanced long at him. "Of
course, you're right. I've made a few token
pleas to take care of the bandit situation but
they've been pap for the voters to make them
believe someone cared. Now that it's real, we're
really going in there, it makes a man think that
there's a hell of a lot to lose here." He went over
to stand by the window. "If Murdo makes a
mistake and gets cut to ribbons down there—"
He turned his head and looked at George Fuller.
"Well, I'd be wasting my time even going back
to the governor's mansion, wouldn't I?"

"You can go back to teaching school," Fuller
said. "It's nice for a man to have a trade to fall
back on."

Stiles stared at him a moment, surprised, then
he laughed, and thrust his hands deep in his
pockets. "Yes, I still know how to pound mathe-
matics into stubborn little heads and warm
bottoms with a cane."

After spending an hour at the pass, Jim
McClintock realized that he needed a horse to get
through; mounted men came and went regularly
and dressed as he was, and mounted, he could
have been passed through as a *bandito*. An
encampment of twenty or thirty guarded the pass,

174

and he knew he could not get past them afoot. And even if he could, getting out with a bag of powder under each arm would be harder than getting in.

He fought down his feeling of frustration then turned back and carefully climbed to the rim where he had left Will Beech.

"Couldn't get through," he said and bellied down, pillowing his head on his crossed arms. "Guards outside the pass too."

"Let's give it up then."

"Maybe we ought to think about it some more," McClintock suggested. He fell silent for a time and Beech waited.

Finally he said, "Jim, I wondered what it would be like if you ever had to give up on a thing."

"Who the hell's give up? I'll just have to think of somethin' else, that's all."

"We're out of grub and our water's gone," Beech said. "Let's hightail it. There was water in the other valley. I'll take my chance on the way to the border." He reached out and took McClintock by the arm. "I'd rather go down fighting my way back, Jim. I mean that."

"Suppose I said no? Suppose I said you had to go it alone?"

"I guess I'd say goodbye then and go," Beech said. "You know, I can make up my mind about a thing too, Jim."

"Looks that way, don't it?" McClintock said. Then he grinned. "All right, we've got about four and a half hours until daylight. Why waste it?"

They started to work their way off the rim, skirting the pass, and they had traveled nearly a half a mile when McClintock stopped suddenly and took cover in a jumble of rocks. Beech opened his mouth to speak but held it when McClintock raised his hand. He cocked his head and listened carefully, then Beech heard it, the sound of horses.

The riders came into view, two *banditos*, one dismounted so he could read the tracks, the small scuffs of sign McClintock had left when he scouted the ridge.

Placing his lips against Beech's ear, McClintock whispered, "No shooting."

They let the *banditos* come on until they were close to them, then McClintock suddenly bounded out, swinging his rifle, butt first. He caught the mounted man squarely on the back of the head and knocked him from the horse and the other bandit whirled and raised his rifle to shoot McClintock.

Beech broke the man's skull with an ax blow and quickly, with great presence of mind, grabbed the reins to keep the horse from bolting. McClintock took a pistol and shell belt from one bandit, and two near full canteens and a bag of meat. Beech got the canteen from the other man, then they mounted quickly and rode on, dropping down toward the valley beyond the pass.

McClintock said, "I figure that's the last bit of luck we'll get from here on in."

"I'm not complaining," Beech said.

They did not hole up after dawn, but rode boldly along the high trails and several times they saw mounted *banditos* some distance away and drew their attention only briefly; dressed in dirty white ducks they were unrecognizable as Americans.

Twice they stopped to rest and in the early evening they took turns dozing in the saddle, and at nightfall they paused on the desert floor and contemplated that last eight miles to Jacob Spaniard's rancho.

Beech asked, "Can we get inside?"

"At night, I think so."

"I guess we've got to go there then." He looked steadily at McClintock. "Is it the girl or do you want to kill Spaniard?"

"Will, I'd like to say it's the girl, but I just don't know."

"We ought to find that out," Beech said and moved out.

When they approached the gate, the sentries on top of the palisade called down to them and McClintock swore arrogantly at them in Spanish and announced that he had a personal message from Calaveras and that the gate must be opened with great speed or he would report their laziness to Spaniard and have them whipped.

There was a scurrying and a few blows struck

and the gates opened. One man came near with a lantern but McClintock and Beech kept their hats pulled low, casting deep black shadows across most of their faces.

Once inside, they rode directly across the huge grounds to the house and dismounted near a side porch. Beech tied the horses and McClintock stomped boldly across the porch, then turned and walked along until he came to a door. He tested it and found it open and stepped inside. The room was dark, but across it he could see a ribbon of light under the door and he made his way there, being careful not to upset anything. In the room there was the strong flavor of tobacco; he supposed it was a study of some kind, a retreat of Spaniard's.

At the door he listened and heard nothing for a moment, then a man coughed gently and a glass clinked as it was touched against a dish. McClintock eased the door open a crack and looked in. Spaniard was in his easy chair, reading, enjoying his cigar and a drink; his back was toward McClintock, who stepped into the room as quietly as fog.

Drawing his pistol, McClintock cocked it slowly, letting the metallic ratcheting of trigger on sear toll the bell of warning in Spaniard's mind.

"You've never been closer to dyin'," McClintock said easily and stepped around where Spaniard could see him, could look into his eyes and know that here was the truth if a man ever spoke it.

The old man sat there for a moment, then reached slowly for his drink. "Stark didn't come back."

"He ain't ever comin' back," McClintock said. He went to the hall door, opened it, whistled softly, and Beech came into the room and closed the door, putting his shoulders against it.

Jacob Spaniard looked at him carefully, then said, "The little man with the fluttering heart. I suspect that you've grown some. Can I offer you a drink?" He reached for the bell pull and stopped when the muscles in McClintock's hand tightened ever so slightly. "Ah, you would shoot me, wouldn't you? And you wouldn't care about the noise." He raised a hand and rubbed his chin thoughtfully. "But a gunshot would bring a dozen men on the run. You know that, don't you?"

"Lock the doors, Will," McClintock said casually and Beech slid the bolt, then walked across the room and locked the connecting door.

"Let's see how quick they get here," McClintock said and the muzzle of his pistol crashed a rosette and exploded the whiskey bottle on Spaniard's table, showering him with whiskey and small shards of glass. Small dots of blood appeared, yet he sat absolutely still as McClintock recocked the pistol.

"Jesus Christ!" Beech said softly and stood slack-jawed, waiting.

EIGHT

Jim McClintock waited, then he heard the rush of feet in the large hall, and Pete Tanner cursed a servant before pounding on the door with his fist. To Spaniard, McClintock spoke softly. "Now you know what to tell him, friend. Tell him plain so that he understands it."

"Cut out that damned pounding!" Spaniard yelled angrily.

"You all right in there?" Tanner asked. "I heard a shot!"

"I was fooling with my gun and it went off," Spaniard said. "Go on and leave me alone."

There was a hesitation, then they could hear Tanner moving away, talking to the servants, his voice and footfalls fading. Will Beech raised a hand and wiped small beads of sweat from his forehead and Jacob Spaniard smiled.

"McClintock, you've got nerve—I'll hand that to you." He raised his hand briefly and let it fall. "Now what?"

"I'm going to ask you one question and I'll ask it once. I don't have to tell you what kind of an answer I want. Is Burkhauser here?"

Spaniard caught his upper lip gently between his teeth and glanced at McClintock's pistol. "Yes, he's here."

"Have him brought to the house, to this room," McClintock ordered. He jerked his head around quickly as someone rapped lightly on the door, then he heard May Spaniard speak and nodded for Beech to open the door.

She stepped inside and started in surprise, then she recognized him and started toward him, but checked herself. Her glance went to her father, who smiled and said, "Your old dad is in a predicament."

"It does seem that way, doesn't it?" She went over to a chair and sat down, carefully folding her flannel robe about her legs.

"We were talking about Sergeant Burkhauser," Will Beech said.

"So you were," Spaniard said. "How are we going to manage it? Neither of you would get across the yard alive. And by the same token, he may not be able to get to the house alive." He spread his hands and shrugged. "What to do? A problem, like I said."

May looked from one to the other, then got up and walked over to a desk; she brought back paper and pen. "Write a note to Tanner, Father. I'll deliver it." She put her hand flat on the paper and looked at Jim McClintock. "But I have a price, Jim. I want him to permit my mother to leave here."

"Can't she just—"

"No, she can't. Do I have your promise?"

"You have it," McClintock said. "Write a nice note, Spaniard."

"Would you shoot me if I don't?"

"Deader than hell."

"In front of my daughter?"

"She can close her eyes," McClintock said flatly.

Spaniard sighed and dipped the pen in the ink pot; he wrote rapidly in a broad hand, then May picked up the note and handed it to McClintock, who read it carefully and gave it back to her.

"I'll get dressed and find Tanner," she said and left the room.

"After you get Burkhauser here," Spaniard said, "just what do you think you can do? Leave? You can't hold me a prisoner in my own house very long." He shook his head gently. "McClintock, you really aren't in charge of anything."

"Then why don't you reach for that bell pull?"

"You'd shoot me."

"That's right."

"But where would you be then?"

"Where would *you* be, Spaniard?" McClintock smiled. "One thing I can count on: you consider yourself more important than me, not worth sacrificing for a man like me. And I just might be fool enough to be willing to die if it meant getting a man like you. That thought's been running through your mind, ain't it?"

"For a fact, it has," Spaniard admitted. "All

right, just how do you figure to manage this?"

"Put your key to the gun room on the desk." He waited and Spaniard produced it; McClintock motioned for Beech to pick it up. "Search his desk for a weapon. Take anything you find."

"I could unload—"

"He'll have spare ammuniton," McClintock said.

Beech rummaged around and found a small derringer and Smith & Wesson pocket .38; he slipped them in his pocket then turned to unlock the door when May knocked. Two Mexican servants helped Finley Burkhauser into the room. One eye was swollen shut and his lips were split, but a smile came into his eyes when he saw McClintock and Will Beech.

"Where the hell you been?" he asked. "Huntin'? Fishin'? Damn it, Jim, you'll never make sergeant."

"Why don't you sit down before you fall down?" McClintock said. "What you been doin'? Pickin' fights again?"

May Spaniard said, "Tanner asked questions. He thinks something's wrong but doesn't know quite what to do about it."

McClintock took off his shell belt and handed it, and the pistol to Burkhauser who had lowered himself in a soft chair. "You keep the lid on here, huh?"

"If a pore in his nose opens," Burkhauser promised, "I'll blow his head off."

"Is there a place where a man could bathe and

shave and change clothes?" McClintock asked.

"There's a tub in my room," May said. "And there's Harry's razor and clothes."

"Don't touch my son's things," Spaniard warned, but McClintock paid no attention to him. He and the girl stepped into the hall; he had his look then followed her quickly to the rear of the house and up a wide flight of stairs. She had an old Mexican woman fetch large buckets of water; he bathed behind a screen and she laid out new clothes and razor and soap.

He dressed and shaved; the clothes were Mexican, expensive, full of fine needle work and inlaid silver. May went out and came back with some more. "Burkhauser is about your size, but the small man is going to be more difficult." She looked at him and forced herself to smile. "How can I say how happy I am to see you alive, Jim?" She was smiling when the tears started and he couldn't believe it even when he watched them spill down her cheeks. Then he stepped to her and she came against him warm and woman soft and he kissed her and it was a wonderful thing, as though it had never happened to him before.

When he put her away from him, he said, "I told Will Beech I didn't know who I came back for, you or your father, but it was you, May. Believe that." Then he put his arm around her and steered her to the door. "Let's give Will a chance to get rid of his fleas."

. . .

Jim McClintock inspected the house from front to back, upstairs and down, and he was convinced that the three of them, well armed, could hold it. All the windows on both floors were barred and the doors were stout oak; a rifle bullet, except from the heaviest buffalo gun would not penetrate them. The house had been intended as a fortress when it was built and he silently thanked Jacob Spaniard for that foresight.

From the gun room, a cell-like cubicle with a steel door, McClintock armed himself with two pistols, a shotgun, and took a heavy-caliber repeating rifle, leaving behind the one he had taken from the *bandito*. He had Beech place shotguns and spare shells in various strategic locations in the house, upstairs and down; Beech and Finley Burkhauser armed themselves well and remained with Spaniard in the study.

Spaniard was under constant guard by one of them and they all had reason to guard him well; McClintock was not concerned about the man escaping for he could be stopped one way or another before he left the house.

May had the cook fix an early meal and it was getting light outside when they sat down in the huge dining hall to eat. McClintock sat at the head of the table, facing the big doors; May sat on his right, then Burkhauser. Jake Spaniard sat across the table, with Will Beech on his left, a vacant chair between them.

"What's the routine of this house?" McClintock asked.

"At sunup, Tanner and Scanlon come in for orders, anything special that needs to be done. And when Stark's here—"

"Stark's dead," McClintock said matter-of-factly.

"Oh. Well, no one will cry about that," May said. "The servants in the house will take my orders."

"Can you trust them?" Beech asked.

"If you mean, will they obey me instead of my father, the answer is yes. The three men in the house have been whipped at one time or another for displeasing him. The women haven't been treated much better."

Finley Burkhauser shook his head and made a clucking sound. "Jake, you just don't know how to get along with people." He glanced at the girl, squinting his good eye. "What about all the riders on the place?"

"The *pistoleros* may follow Tanner and Scanlon. But I don't think the others will. Money is the loyalty here, Mr. Burkhauser. There is no love. Everything has been built with money and fear."

One of the servants came in and spoke in Spanish: "Señor Tanner approaches the house. Señor Scanlon is with him."

"Vah-moose," McClintock said in his accent.

"Take the women to the kitchen. Will, guard the back door. May, go show them in here but don't come in with 'em. You hear that?"

"Yes," she said and left the table.

Jacob Spaniard wiped his lips with a napkin. "Your reign, gentlemen, will be short. They know something is wrong and will be ready for it."

"You think I'm goin' to be pickin' my teeth?" Burkhauser asked, dropping a hand casually to his lap and keeping it there; he let the other rest idly on the table since the function of the arm hadn't been restored.

The big doors opened and Scanlon stepped inside first; he had a pistol in his hand and Tanner crowded past him, then they both stopped. "Wellwellwell," Scanlon said, smiling. "I just knew somethin' was up when you had the old man taken from his cell." His glance fastened on Jim McClintock. "I halfway figured you was Injun enough to give the *banditos* the slip. Comes to my mind now that you and the old man fought it out with a bunch on the Rio Salado sometime back and came off best. Calaveras still cusses about that."

"What the hell is this, a social hour?" Tanner asked. "You just ease out of the line of fire, Mr. Spaniard."

"Sit!" McClintock said flatly. He had his fingers lightly laced together and Tanner saw that and smiled.

"You pretty fast with a pistol, fella? I never heard anything about that."

Harry Scanlon cocked his pistol although he still had the muzzle pointing slightly down, and Burkhauser said, "Raise that and you're a dead man."

"Aw," Scanlon said and laughed. "You're bluffin' me, old man. One good eye, one good arm, you're just bluffin'."

"Better believe me," Burkhauser warned. "Let the hammer down easy."

For a moment Scanlon was motionless, then he said, "I'll let it down on a cap," and thrust the pistol out like it was a stick and he was going to poke something with it.

The crash of Burkhauser's pistol was slightly muffled and the concussion made the tablecloth jump, then Scanlon flapped both hands to his breast, took one staggering step and fell on his face.

There was a stunned instant there when Tanner did not move and Jim McClintock said, "Do it now if you want to!"

Jacob Spaniard's face was chalk and he kept his lips compressed tightly. Pete Tanner waited, his palm an inch from his holstered pistol; he watched McClintock and Burkhauser. McClintock would have to draw and half turn before he fired, but Burkhauser likely had his gun recocked for the second shot.

Tanner let his breath go and his shoulders

rounded, his arms going loose and lifeless. "All right, who wants to die quick anyway?" He reached out with his foot and rolled Scanlon on his back; the bullet had struck the center of his breastbone and broken his back. "It's funny how much older a man looks when he's dead, don't it? What am I goin' to do? Stand here 'til I take root?" He laughed. "If I did it'd be the first roots I ever put down. Since I've been sixteen I've spent more time in jail than out."

"You can turn and ride out of here if you take the *pistoleros* with you," McClintock said evenly, "And you won't get a better deal than that anywhere."

"Go back to Texas?" Tanner shook his head. "It wouldn't be three weeks before some hick sheriff spotted me. Besides, if the *pistoleros* left here, Calaveras would be down on you in a week. All that's ever stood him off is those cannon out there and the men inside the wall."

"You old fool," Spaniard said, "why don't you shut your mouth?"

Tanner looked at him steadily for a moment, then laughed. "Mr. Spaniard, you've just got to stop thinkin' everyone is stupid." He put his attention back on Burkhauser. "What's the chance of makin' a deal with the State of Texas?"

"What could I promise you?" Burkhauser asked.

"You could talk for me. You've got more pull than a team of mules. Burkhauser, I've got ten

189

years waitin' for me. If I could get that cut to five I'd—"

"You'd what?" McClintock asked.

"I'd throw in with you," Tanner said. "The *pistoleros* take my orders. I could get you to the border."

Jacob Spaniard swore softly. "Pete, where's your guts? Hell, Burkhauser will promise you anything and lie his way out of it!"

Slowly Pete Tanner swung his eyes to him. "I never heard of him breakin' his word. And I never knew you to really keep yours. Well, Burkhauser? What can we do? All I've got left to bargain with is my life, the few years I have left. And that's precious to a man like me."

"I'd do my best for you, right down the line," Burkhauser said. "There's my word on that."

"Good enough for me," Tanner said.

"Pete, you'd turn your back on me?" Spaniard asked. "I broke you out of prison, made you into somebody important. You'd turn your back on what I've done?"

"There's somethin' about dyin' in Texas, when I come down to thinkin' about it, that just plain appeals to me. What's got to be done?"

"We want to get back across the border," McClintock said. "There's three of us and the two women. I don't think we ought to waste much time about it since Calaveras is liable to come out of the hills any time now."

"With thirty heavily armed *pistoleros,* good horses, and light wagons, we stand a good chance of makin' it," Tanner said. "What about him?" He nodded toward Spaniard.

"He comes too," Burkhauser said.

"Let him stay," McClintock said.

Burkhauser frowned. "You arguin' with me?"

"Tellin' you this time, Finley. He bought what he wanted here, then let him have it."

"I didn't expect sympathy from you," Spaniard said.

"You think that's what it is?" McClintock got up slowly. "Is there any reason we can't be movin' by noon?"

"None I can rightly think of," Tanner admitted. He turned to the door and stopped there. "The girl might not want to leave him. The old lady, well, she's been a prisoner of her own mind for so long—" He let the rest trail off. "It's your worry, not mine. I'll keep my end of the bargain. That's all I can handle."

Spaniard said, "Isn't there one decent man on the face of this damned earth? One man another can trust?"

Tanner looked at him and grinned. "Jake, do you know what you're talkin' about?" He shook his head and walked out, closing the door.

Spaniard started to get up but McClintock said, "Sit down." He went to the door and whistled and Will Beech came from the back of the house. May Spaniard had been standing at the head of the stair; she came down and stepped inside when McClintock did. Beech looked at Scanlon, then went over to a sideboard, took a drape off it and covered the dead man.

"Where's Tanner?" he asked, looking around.

"Getting ready to leave," McClintock said. He touched May on the arm. "Can you have your mother packed and ready to travel in an hour? Go light. We're going to move as fast as we can. Don't take anything you can't put in two suitcases."

"We'll take what's on our backs," she said, then raised up and kissed him lightly. "Thank you, Jim." She turned to the door and stopped and looked back at her father. "Goodbye, and I'm sorry."

"You ought to be," Spaniard said.

"She's sorry for you," Beech said with some disgust. "Go on, girl, get your things ready. I never liked this place from the first moment I saw it."

McClintock left Burkhauser to guard Spaniard; he and Beech went outside and found Pete Tanner. "There's no sense in leavin' anything for Calaveras," McClintock said. "Is there any way those cannon can be spiked?"

"Plug the muzzles with mud and blow 'em up," Tanner suggested.

"Where's the powder magazine?"

"In those blockhouses on each side of the main gate."

McClintock thought about it a moment. "Tell you what; clear out all the Mexicans except the *pistoleros*. Better have them stay by the stable. I want four or five kegs of powder placed at the base of the wall near the corner blockhouses. Set a box of fuses at the base too. I can fire into them from the porch. I want to blow up the powder magazines too."

"Be a lot better," Tanner said, "if we just got the hell out and let Calaveras have the cannon and fodder."

"So he could blow the hell out of some town just before his raiders swooped down?" McClintock shook his head. "You set the charges, Tanner. When you come to the house I'll set them off."

"All right, you're runnin' the whole shebang." He walked away and McClintock and Beech went over to where the *pistoleros* were working. There were eight or ten Americans; the rest were Mexican, all well dressed and heavily armed. There wasn't a man among them who didn't know who McClintock was but none asked questions.

"Jake Spaniard is under arrest," McClintock said, speaking to none in particular. "You take orders from me, or from Pete Tanner. There's a hundred dollars for every man who gets his horse's forefeet wet in the Rio Grande."

One of the Americans said, "What about his hindfeet, Ranger?"

"I said the forefeet. I'll be payin' off while the wagon crosses with the women."

They looked at each other, then one said, "Sounds good to me."

Beech and McClintock walked back to the house. May had come down with her mother, a slight, pale woman who kept glancing about as though frightened. McClintock said, "We're goin' to take you home, ma'am. Don't be afraid now." He touched Beech lightly. "You take care of her, stay with her." He left them and went into the study where Burkhauser held a gun on Jacob Spaniard. He stepped up to Spaniard and said, "Where do you keep your money?"

"Not here," Spaniard said.

McClintock knotted his fist and pulped the man's nose, driving him and his chair over backward. Then he stepped around and looked down. "One last time: I want money for your wife. You tell me or I'll stomp you here and now."

Spaniard pawed at the blood on his face, then pointed to the bookcase. "Behind it—safe."

McClintock fisted the man's shirt and dragged him over; he pushed the bookcase aside and exposed the safe door. "Open it up! Count out ten or fifteen thousand and put it in a sack." He kicked Spaniard in the ribs. "Goddammit! Move!"

There was a moment of fooling with the dial, then the door opened and Spaniard set some leather bags on the floor. "There's twenty thousand," he said.

He grabbed McClintock by the pant leg, to hold him, but the Ranger jerked his leg free and hefted the two bags. "You keep watch on him, Finley."

He went out and gave the money to Beech, who simply stared at it, but asked no questions. Pete Tanner was coming toward the porch when McClintock stepped outside, rifle in the crook of his arm. "Is everything set, Tanner?" He could plainly see the powder kegs and boxes of fuses. "The people out of here?"

"Just like you wanted," Tanner said.

McClintock went to the edge of the porch and sat down, crossing his legs. He sighted carefully, touched off the .45-70 and watched the corner blockhouse erupt in a cloud of smoke and flying adobe. The concussion broke some of the second-story windows, and he shifted, fired again, and blew up the other blockhouse. The mangled cannon whirled and fell and the dust rose thick and choking, drifting across the yard slowly.

His third shot went into the powder magazine and the blast bowled him over; he got up, dusted off his clothes, and went into the house. The commotion in the study drew him and he found Spaniard sitting on the floor, cursing, holding his aching head with both hands.

Burkhauser shrugged. "I belted him a little; he ain't really hurt much. You blow up a thing or two, boy?"

"Celebratin' the Fourth of July a little early," McClintock admitted. "You still want to stay here, Spaniard?"

"It's take a chance with the *banditos* or the State of Texas," Burkhauser told him. "You got a minute to decide." He looked around at the lavish tapestries and carved furniture and inlaid tile floor. "The trouble with you, Spaniard, is that you've never had to fight for a damned thing in your life. You were born with a silver soup dish in your mouth and you lived off the sweat of your servants until you were a grown man and when it all vanished in the bust, you just never could admit that it was gone. Then you had it lucky and hit it rich and every damned stick of this was built with another man's sweat, and held against the bandits with another man's gun. But you've just seen the last of the easy life, Jake. You're goin' to do somethin' you never did before. You're goin' to stay here and fight for this place."

"Aw, come on, Finley," McClintock cut in. "There's no time—"

"Ain't there?" Burkhauser arched an eyebrow. "Jim, I never knew you to fool yourself. And I never knew you to make a mistake in judgment about me. There's a lot of miles and the river and the *banditos* between here and Texas. Odds are fair-to-middlin' that we'd make it, but damn it all, it's like shootin' up a belt of ammunition and not hittin' nothin'. Jake Spaniard wouldn't be in a

196

Texas jail where he belongs, and Calaveras would be free to go on raidin'." He shook his head. "That ain't what we was sent here for, Jim. You know it too."

"There are other things to think about."

"The girl? Sure. Don't blame you there. But we've never been in a position before that would make Calaveras come to us and I say we shouldn't pass this up. We can defend this place, boy."

"I kind of get the notion," McClintock said, "that you're puttin' that from the sergeant to the corporal sort of."

"If I have to do it that way, then I will," Burkhauser said. "Jim, I don't relish the idea of dyin' here, in company like Spaniard, but I took an oath, same as you. We stay."

McClintock sighed. "I guess argument wouldn't do any good. But I don't like puttin' a gun in Spaniard's hand."

"He needs us, but we don't need him," Burkhauser said. "Calaveras would roast him over a low fire and he knows it."

Before darkness, many of the Mexicans who had run when they saw there was trouble came back. They had no place to go and this was their home. Rather than die at the hands of Calaveras they elected to help and were taken into the house. There were two priests among them and they came back to administer last rites to those who were bound to fall. The arrival of the Mexican workers crowded the house, yet he was glad they had come back for they could load weapons and perform other chores and free the *pistoleros* for the fighting.

Every container that would hold water had been filled and placed inside the house and there was enough food to last them three weeks. Countermanding Burkhauser's order, McClintock left the horses in the corral; it was either the horses in the house or the Mexican workers, so he really had no choice at all.

He had Tanner push the wagons and two wheeled carts together in the yard and burn them; he wanted none of them loaded with hay, set afire and pushed against the house.

It was liable to get hot enough as it was.

There was no window or gun aperture unmanned by a *pistolero* and the women were taken to rooms in the center of the house where no stray bullet could reach them.

Sundown brought a cooling breeze.

They ate in shifts, then a sentry signaled down that a large band of mounted men were approaching. They came over the rubble of the wall and on toward the burning wagons; McClintock could see them clearly and he recognized Calaveras although it was the first look at the man he had ever had. The bandit was mounted on a splendid horse and his saddle was laden with silver, polished discs that threw back the bright firelight.

To Burkhauser, McClintock said, "Let's go parley. On the porch though. Will, you stand by the door, ready to let us in if we have to jump fast. Tanner, be ready to shoot if I tell you to."

He left his place by the window and opened the door, stepping out, Burkhauser a pace behind him. Calaveras stopped, looked at them, then came on alone while his men crowded into the yard.

When he was near, he squinted at them curiously, then spoke in fair English. "I have not seen you before." He had a high voice, thickly accented. "You have names, no?"

"I'm McClintock. This is Burkhauser. We're—"

"Soooo?" Calaveras said, letting his tone rise. "You have fought my *banditos*, eh? It is not a thing Calaveras will ever forget." He waved his hand to indicate his men. "It is a bad day for you that we should meet. I can promise you that."

"What do you want here?" Burkhauser asked.

"I have grown tired of the hills. From the mountains I can see this beautiful rancho and I say to myself, Calaveras, why do you not take it. Spaniard has had it long enough." He smiled and brushed his thick mustache. "So I bring my men. It is not the right thing?"

"Did Stark ever make it to your camp?" McClintock asked.

"Ah, so it was you who sent him? You killed my men, no?"

"As dead as I could," McClintock admitted. "And maybe a few more before this is done." He spoke without turning his head. "The door, Will. Shoot, Tanner!"

He knocked Burkhauser inside and followed him, rolling over as Beech and another man slammed the door. Tanner was firing and the *pistoleros* laid down a volley that wiped twenty men off their horses. Calaveras's horse stumbled and fell and by some miracle he rolled free as it fell and dashed back across the yard while bullets sprinkled around him. The *banditos* deployed to the rubble of the wall and the firing began to die down.

The waiting game began.

McClintock went around and found that no one was hurt. He did not expect much activity until dawn but made sure that lookouts were always on duty and he had three *pistoleros* keep rifles trained on the well since he meant to deny Calaveras the use of it.

He went to May's room; her mother was sleeping and they stepped into the hall so as not to wake her. Gently McClintock put his arm around her; he held her and stroked her hair, then said, "I guess Finley was right; we wouldn't have made it to the border. It was just something I wanted bad enough to believe it was possible."

"Don't blame yourself for anything, Jim. Where's Father?"

"Downstairs. With a gun. Fighting for his place." She looked at him oddly and he smiled and kissed her. "Finley thinks it's bad for a man to die without a reason. Or maybe it's just that he don't like to see a man go through life without ever really payin' for anythin'. To me it don't matter. But then I think of you and it does." He leaned against the wall and lit a cigar. "In the years I've served Texas, I sort of figured I'd go out belly down in some gully, tryin' to uphold what I believed in. The thought of it never scared me none and it seemed a good way to go, for somethin', you know. But I guess it's really a hell of a way, May. You know what I mean. There has to be more to a man than himself, more to livin' than for himself. A man has to dedicate himself to more than one thing. You get just one idea in mind and you turn out like your father. May, you know what I want? I want us to go get the priest and have him marry us." He waited for her to say something and when she didn't, he looked at her. "That sound so bad you can't think of an answer?"

"It didn't sound bad at all," she said. "I'd want to put on a good dress though. Something I've been saving for—" She quickly put her arms around his waist and buried her face in the front of his shirt. "I want there to be a tomorrow, Jim! I want there to be a next year too!"

"Seems like I never get around to doin' a thing until it's too late," he said. "But I want to marry you, May. May? Did you hear me?"

She raised her head and looked at him, then released him and moved slightly back. "I won't take long. Will you bring him up here?"

"Yes," he said and waited until she went back in the room before going down the stairs.

He found the priest in the kitchen, eating; the man spoke no English and McClintock explained what he wanted, then he went out. Will Beech was at a station near the front door; Burkhauser and Jacob Spaniard were farther down, and Burkhauser said, "Upstairs, downstairs, can't you settle down?"

"Just arrangin' for my weddin'," McClintock said.

"The hell!" Beech said. "You can pick the damndest times, Jim."

"Married," Burkhauser murmured and smiled. "You just never get enough trouble do you? Bandits on the outside and you want to get married." He looked at Jacob Spaniard, who had said nothing. "You're goin' to have to call him Daddy. That ought to make any man think twice." Then he got up and put his rifle aside. "I'd kinda like to stand up there with you, boy. You know, all we've been through and that. It may be the last danged thing I'll ever ask you, Jim. What ya say?"

"I guess that's what I stopped to ask you," McClintock said, and went on up the stairs.

NINE

The predawn hours were entirely silent.

Jim McClintock woke and lay perfectly still, conscious of May's warmth beside him. Gently he moved away from her and got out of bed to dress and she stirred, then sat up. "Jim?"

"It's all right," he said softly. "Four hour honeymoon wasn't very long, was it?" He bent and kissed her and pulled the blanket up around her neck. "Stay here. Will you do that for me?"

"What are you going to do?"

"They'll need me downstairs. Be daylight in another hour."

She wanted him to stay; he knew that but there was no time for it. He buckled on his pistols and went out of her room and down the hall to the stairs. Burkhauser was in the library, squatting by one of the windows; the oak shutters were closed and he peered out a rifle port.

So quietly did McClintock come up that Burkhauser started, then he grinned and said, "Damn it, will you cut out that soft walkin' around me?"

"You still of the mind that Calaveras can't break into the house?"

"Nope, but I'm sure it'll cost him dear."

"With a little luck I could make it out of here, get a horse and make it to the border," McClintock said. "I don't see any other chance, Finley. To me it's just a question of time. A couple days of this and Calaveras is going to make it in. There never was a fort built that wouldn't fall. Ain't that what you've said from time to time?"

"That was just talk," Burkhauser admitted.

"The hell it was. You goin' to help me sneak out or not?"

Burkhauser studied him for a long moment. "You've thought it out?" McClintock nodded. "I know you're right, Jim, but I don't want to say it or admit it. Boy, I put you down as the best friend I ever had. If you was my own son I—"

"Aw, now don't get blubbery," McClintock said with unusual gruffness. "If I'm goin' I've got to get at it." He started to get up, then changed his mind. "All right, I admit it; I came when you whistled because I liked you. And don't bother to tell me why."

"Well, I was right all along, wasn't I?"

"Nobody ever wins an argument with you," McClintock said. Then he smiled, got up and walked to the rear of the house where Will Beech had a station. He took off one of his gunbelts, rolled it around the holster and laid it aside and put his coat over it.

Beech watched him a moment, then said, "What are you doing?"

"Gettin' ready to leave. Give me five minutes before you say anything."

"It wouldn't do any good if I tried to stop you, would it?"

"You won't," McClintock said, "because you know I'm doing the right thing. Kill the lamps." He waited until the room was dark, then quietly opened the door and slipped out. The cool breeze surprised him; with the house tightly closed up he had not been aware of any wind at all.

He stayed in the deep shadows and looked at the yard; it was eighty yards to the wall and the buildings along it, but the night was dark enough and he could belly along as good as any Indian. When he left the porch he did so by simply rolling off, then he inched along, barely moving his arms and legs; his destination was the garden, a plot of greenery forty yards away, so he continued to crawl along, not knowing whether or not Calaveras had men stationed along the wall. It was McClintock's guess that most of the *banditos* had pulled back to their camp along the rubble in the front of the house.

He reached the garden and hidden by the stalks of corn, moved quickly along toward the southeast corner. There was a cluster of small adobe huts there, homes of the Mexicans who worked around the ranch house, and McClintock figured that the *banditos* wouldn't bother to watch this part of the yard.

At the edge of the garden patch he paused to look around and saw nothing, no movement, no sign of life. Thirty yards at best, he judged, and debated whether to walk it or run it. He decided to walk and stepped out with a measured pace and he didn't take a decent breath until he reached the first adobe. In the deep shadows he stopped and gathered together his frayed nerves, took a few deep breaths, then jumped up and caught a ridge pole so he could swing to the roof. Ten seconds later he was atop the wall and over, dropping lightly to the ground.

It was a strange, frightening feeling to stand there with the wind on him and the desert and mountains and the river before him. He waited only briefly, then worked his way around the wall until he came to the crumbled litter of the blockhouse. His way became the Indian's way then, blending with the shadows, moving like a breath, silently, without revealing himself.

He found the horse herd and worked his way into it; they were picketed on ground ropes and he could easily have taken one, but a hard core of stubbornness rose in him and he searched out the horse belonging to Calaveras. He found it, guarded, on a picket, and he worked his way close, taking his time about it and making no sound at all. Twenty yards away the *banditos* slept in clusters around their dead fires; they would wake at the slightest sound;

the first mistake he made would be his last.

McClintock moved so close he could smell sweat and tobacco on the guard, then his arm came around the man's throat like two oak sticks clamped together and the knife went in clean and McClintock held the man, shutting off his cry until the life went out of him.

Then he lowered him gently to the ground, untied the horse and carefully, slowly, led him past the herd and then mounted up. The horse was magnificent, a white stallion sixteen hands at least, with a deep chest and long legs and a proud, arched nose. Riding bareback, McClintock held the horse until he was well clear, then let him run, let him use that splendid power.

He was four miles away at dawn, and with this horse, this much of a start, he did not fear any pursuit by the *banditos*. He was, though, sorry that he couldn't hear Calaveras rave when he discovered the horse was gone.

May slept until the first touch of sun came through her window and then she sat up in bed, letting the sheet fall away from her, letting the sun touch her. Dressing, she thought it strange that she could feel so serene, as though the *banditos* were not surrounding the house at all, as though she had only to go downstairs now and fix breakfast for her husband.

Firing began when some of the *banditos* tried to

reach the well and were driven back by the *pistoleros*, then it grew quiet again and May went to the back of the house, thinking Jim McClintock might be there. She found Will Beech and several *pistoleros*, then turned without speaking and walked toward the front of the house.

Her father was there, dozing, his head touching his chest; he had a Winchester across his lap and when he heard her step he looked up. "What are you doing down here?" he asked.

"Looking for my husband."

He laughed softly. "Do you think that's anything to gloat about? Because you married a man who figured he was going to die anyway and thought it would be nice to sleep with you first? He's gone."

She stared at him, her expression angry and hurt. "What do you mean, he's gone?"

"I heard Beech and Burkhauser talking about it. He skedaddled about an hour before dawn. What's the matter, May? Your husband keeping secrets from you already?"

She did not hear Burkhauser's step, but his voice pulled her head around. "Spaniard, why don't I just shoot you? Is there anything you don't hate?" He came up to her and took her by the arm and led her to the kitchen where the Mexican servants were fixing breakfast. He made her sit down and poured some coffee for her. "He had to go, girl, because he was the only one. Do you understand?"

"I understand that he's gone, that I had him and lost him," she said. "There was no one else?"

"No one. He's as good as any Injun," Burkhauser said. "I've always figured myself better than most when it comes to makin' no tracks, but Jim's the best of anyone I've seen. He's the only one who could get out and have any chance at all of makin' it."

"And when he does get to the river, then what?"

"He'll bring Texas Rangers back with him, a whole company maybe. They'll come, legal or not. They'll come because they're Texans." He sighed and wiped a hand across his beard stubble. "We'll hold out somehow. A couple of days more anyway. Three if we have a little luck. You see, Calaveras will take the well. He's bound to. Tonight maybe. He's lost four or five men tryin' it in the daylight and he's too smart to lose more. Sooner or later he's goin' to get the idea of pushin' some rubble ahead of his men while they belly up and when he reaches the well, others will come up and they'll build a wall of rubble between the well and the house and then drink all they danged please."

"He may not think of that."

"He'll think of it," Burkhauser insisted. "And once their canteens are full, he'll start pushin' rubble toward the porch or some side of the house. Fort against fort; that's the way it'll be. You see, in this kind of warfare, it's the dash across the open that's bad. Once that's cut up with trenches or shell holes, or some kind of protection, why it's only a matter of time before we're breeched. The Injuns used their buffalo hide shields; they'd turn a 50-caliber bullet unless hit dead center." He reached out and patted her hand. "You've got a good man in Jim McClintock, and I'm happy to say he's got a good woman. It wouldn't surprise me none if you both lived to have kids."

"You're a very nice man, Mr. Burkhauser."

"I can name a few who'd disagree with that." He patted her hand again and got up. "Drink your coffee and think about the time when Jim will be back. Don't borrow trouble."

"You're right. He'll be back."

"Jim's got a head on him, and he's got a lot of nerve. He knows how to suck juice out of a dry branch. He'll make it to the river all right."

"Mr. Burkhauser, are you trying to convince yourself a little?"

He smiled. "Well, I guess. I don't have the faith most have."

McClintock dismounted and walked the horse for a mile, then to save him further and to make time, he began to dogtrot, a loose-legged run he had learned from the Indians and he kept it up for two miles, then mounted and let the stallion set his own pace, a long mile eating trot.

Toward noon McClintock found a seep and scooped away the sand to get to a pool of water no bigger than the brim of his hat. He drank, watered the horse, then rode on, watching the desert for any sign of the Mexican army.

In midafternoon he saw a rise of distant dust and altered his course, meaning to skirt them wide. It meant a great waste of time, perhaps as much as five hours and he cursed this run of bad luck but he had no choice.

He estimated that there were nearly a hundred troops from the size of the dust raised and he worked to the west, trying to keep out of their way for if their scouts picked him up, he knew he couldn't outrun them.

The sun kept settling and the cavalry kept coming on while he swung well out of their way and finally he began to put them behind him and felt a vast relief. Then he stopped and cocked his head, thinking that his hearing was playing tricks on him. But it came again, the faint tones of a cavalry "C" horn. There was no mistaking it at all and he wheeled the stallion around and drew his pistol, firing it into the air as fast as he could roll the hammer under his thumb.

As he rode toward the cavalry he could see scouts coming toward him; twenty minutes brought them together and he couldn't remember when dirty-shirt blue had ever looked better. A sergeant was in charge and he took McClintock directly to Major Murdo; the command was halted and the troopers had been dismounted. McClintock saw the wagons and artillery but there was no time to ask questions about it.

Murdo gave him a canteen and sent a trooper to take care of the horse. An orderly brought out camp stools and they sat down in the shade of a quartermaster wagon.

"The last person I expected to meet," Murdo said, "was a Texas Ranger. We ran across two troops of Mexican cavalry earlier today. For a time there I thought we were going to have to show our carbines to get through." He smiled and offered the canteen again. "I know that you're not out here prospecting. A little trouble?"

"The *banditos* have Spaniard's place surrounded. Burkhauser is forted up inside the house with the *pistoleros*, but Calaveras will surely try to storm the place soon. It's just a question of time, Major."

"By God, you're handing me that bandit on a platter! Captain Randolph!" He chuckled and offered McClintock one of his cigars. "I rather figured on going into the mountains after him."

"Well, sir, if he gets wind you're comin', you'll sure have to go into the mountains. He'll vanish like a woman's blush."

The captain came up, clutching his saber to

keep it from thrashing against his leg. He saluted and waited for Murdo to speak. He looked at McClintock who was taking another pull at the canteen.

"Randolph, take two companies and mount immediately. I want you to make a night march of it, quick time." He made a circle of his arms. "At dawn I want you to be ready to move into Spaniard's hacienda. McClintock will mark out a route on your maps. We'll drive straight on with the artillery and wagons. Now this is important: hold back, well out of sight of Calaveras until we attack him. He'll see that we're not a large force and try to overwhelm us. You can charge and cut off his chance of retreat."

"Good plan, sir. We'll be riding in fifteen minutes."

"Make it ten. McClintock, will you go with Randolph and give him a route?"

"Sure thing," McClintock said and followed the captain back to his command. Randolph got out his map case and McClintock showed him the exact location of the hacienda.

"Close to the mountains, isn't it?" Randolph said. "That might be a good spot to wait for the show to commence." He put his finger on the pass. "How many men would it take to hold that? We have two Gatling guns on light carriages."

"They could hold the pass. A squad I'd say."

"I think we'd better do that. Let me take it up with the major."

McClintock waited, smoking his cigar. The first sergeant stood nearby, then he came over, his jaws gently working his cud of tobacco. "Ain't I seen you before?"

"How the hell would I know?"

"Sure, last year on the Neuces, when they had that fence cuttin' trouble." He took off his glove and extended his hand. "Reilly's the name. You're McClintock. Where's that old geezer that was with you?"

"The *banditos* kind of got him tied up for a spell."

The sergeant shook his head. "Poor *banditos*. He's sure hell on wheels. I still hear talk from some of the old timers who remember him in the Army. What the hell you guys doin' in Mexico? Ain't that against the law?"

"He wanted to pick wild flowers. Got a weakness for 'em."

"All right, so it's none of my business." He went back to his place when Randolph and Murdo came back.

"The captain has a good idea," Murdo said. "I'll move the whole command and send the Gatling guns and two squads on to the pass. Calaveras will break of course and we'll pursue. When they open up on him from the pass we'll have him boxed."

"Major, did you ever fight *banditos* before?"

"No, I never did."

"They're worse'n Apaches. You're goin' to lead some empty saddles back to the river."

"I don't expect it'll be a ball, McClintock. But we'll get what we came after, Mexican army or not." He turned to Randolph. "See that the Gatling guns move out immediately. McClintock, you could use a meal; I think we have time for that." He took him by the arm, and led him back to his command post.

Calaveras started moving his men up; they pushed large hunks of adobe before them and the rifle fire from the house did little damage. When he reached the well his men took cover behind the curbing and the adobe was erected into a small wall and other men bellied forward, pushing blocks and this went on until he had a barricade four foot high and twenty foot wide between the well and the house.

Calaveras had solved his problem of being thirsty.

The shooting from the house died off; there was no sense in wasting ammunition peppering the barricade.

The noon sun seemed to hang in the sky, melting there, then it passed on, dropping down. Many of Calaveras's men were moving up to the well, each man bringing with him a chunk of adobe and toward evening they began their advance across the yard, an inch by inch crawl, nudging their cover ahead of them.

Inside, Burkhauser ordered that no lamps be lighted when darkness fell and went upstairs to speak to May; he wanted to make certain she did not leave her room.

She was not there and he stood in the hall a moment, then she opened a door farther down and he walked toward her. "Won't you come in, please?" She stood aside for him and he stepped in, sweeping off his hat. Jacob Spaniard's wife sat in a high-backed chair, reading; she looked at him and closed her book and put it aside.

"Sit down, Mr. Burkhauser. Will you have some wine?"

"Thank you, no," he said. "I came to warn you not to leave your room tonight. There seems no doubt that Calaveras will try to breech the house tonight."

The old woman looked at him a long moment, then said, "Mr. Burkhauser, are there only desperate men in this world?"

He frowned. "I don't think I understand, ma'am."

"Will you sit down?"

"Only for a moment, thank you." He crossed his legs and eased his arm and waited.

"May, would you pour me some wine? I asked you, Mr. Burkhauser, if there were any men in the world who were not desperate. Are there men who can defer to others without feeling that they have lost their honor? Are there men in the world who act from kindness and not desperation, afraid that they will expose some sign of weakness? What is it about weakness that you fear, Mr. Burkhauser?" She spread her frail hands in a simple gesture. "Once you were kind to me and my children. I've never forgotten that, and I thought that here is a man who is not driven by forces he cannot control. But I was wrong, wasn't I? You're as relentless as Jacob, aren't you?"

"Yes," Burkhauser said. "And Calaveras." He thought about it for a time. "I suppose it would be easy to blame it all on time and place, because it's such a big country and a man is always pretty much on his own. He just feels that he'll do what he wants and if someone don't like it, then get out of the way. But I wouldn't say that about myself; I don't need that excuse. I think what I do is right. I think it's for good. And I don't mean to budge an inch." He stood up slowly. "I have to get back. But before I go I'd like to say somethin'. You want a man not driven by a force he can't control? You think that's a good man?" He shook his head. "Jake would have amounted to somethin' if he'd ever learned to rule himself and not be driven. I've known many like him. They get to a point where they can't tell good or bad, right or wrong. Maybe they never could." He bowed slightly.

"Thank you for the talk. Again I warn you not to leave your room tonight." He stepped to the door and went out and he had taken a half dozen steps before he realized that May had followed him out.

"Don't blame her," she said.

He smiled. "Why would I do that? She's a product now of Jake Spaniard. What she was has been lost long ago, perhaps when she got on the train to go East." He studied her face intently. "But you, he's never done that to you. Not like her or Harry. Why?"

"Because," she said, "I'm as desperate as he. Desperate not to be the kind of person he is."

She went back with her mother and Burkhauser walked down the wide stairs. Pete Tanner came from the rear of the house; they stopped in the hallway to talk.

"There's some of Calaveras's men camped on the porch. I guess we can keep 'em off the roof though." Tanner brushed his dense mustache. "It wasn't so bad, holdin' 'em off at a distance, but when they move in, you just can't get a shot at 'em. They crouch down along the walls and you can't even see 'em."

Burkhauser compressed his lips and nodded grimly. "That's our weak spot all right; we can't shoot out and they can jam a rifle through the ports and shoot in. Tell you what though. We could make it pretty hot on that porch come

218

morning. For the time being, keep everyone near the walls. Keep the movin' around to a minimum."

"I don't feel like sittin' here and bein' potted at," Tanner said.

"Tanner, you've been throwin' lead all your life, so I don't see how you've got a right to complain 'cause a little's comin' your way now."

"I've just got to be doin' somethin', that's all."

"Then why don't you go in the kitchen and make some coffee?"

"Aw, can't you ever talk sense?" Tanner asked before walking away.

As soon as darkness fell, Calaveras made his bid to break into the house. Four of his most daring horsemen carried the ram, a huge ridge pole taken from one of the other buildings. They carried it in a rope sling and rode madly toward the huge front door, braving the rifle fire from the house, and by some miracle they made it, swooping in the ram, crashing it against the door, shaking the entire house. The bolts holding the cross bar started to give and Burkhauser ordered a large, heavy barricade built across the hall and he put Spaniard and a dozen *pistoleros* there, waiting for the time when the door would give and the *banditos* would spill in.

The second run against the door was not too successful; one of the riders was downed and the pole went askew, upsetting another rider and causing a horse to go down. The pole went onto the porch, rolled crossways into the yard and it had to be taken away before another four men could make a run for the door.

This took time, moving a barricade up to protect the *banditos*, then moving it back so the riders could get a clear tilt at the porch.

The third attempt tore half the lag screws from the hinges, and Burkhauser knew that one more good one would bring it crashing down. Calaveras knew it too for he massed a body of men behind the barricades, ready to charge the minute the door gave.

Another pole was brought up, and this time six horsemen carried it; if one or two fell, enough would remain to guide the butt into the target. They thundered across the yard, braving the rifle fire, and one was hit; he fell while the others came on and the pole shot out, smashing against the door.

Splinters flew and the massive door teetered and fell in, jarring the house when it crashed to the floor. Instantly the doorway was filled with *banditos* and the *pistoleros* fired in volley, standing upright behind their barricade. The range was ten yards and men fell and the room was choking with powder smoke, then the doorway was empty; Calaveras had pulled his men back and the silence was a pain to the ears.

Two of the *pistoleros* were dead and a third pinched an arm to try to stop the bleeding where a bullet had passed through it. Jacob Spaniard lay crumbled on the floor; the bullet had struck him just above the left eye and there was very little bleeding.

From the left end of the barricade, Pete Tanner breathed heavily and absent-mindedly punched fresh shells into his repeater. He stepped back and empty cartridge cases rolled under his feet.

Finley Burkhauser was on his knees, one hand bracing himself, the other pressed to his right breast; blood seeped between his tightly held fingers and Tanner swore and came over, kneeling down.

"Bad?"

Burkhauser looked at him and managed a smile. "Worse'n a cold, I'll tell you that."

There was blood on his lips and Tanner saw pink froth at his nostrils and knew that a lung had been punctured.

"Hadn't you better stretch out or somethin'? I'll get Beech."

"No," Burkhauser said. "We've got to guard the rest of the house." He clutched Tanner's arm for support. "We'll hold the door with what we have here. Can't do anythin' else, Pete. Calaveras is goin' to lose men too. More'n we are. That door's just so wide. Can only get so many through at a time." He raised his eyes and looked at Tanner. "What the hell ever started you on the owlhoot anyway?"

"Long story. You've heard it before. Poor people. Got tired of it. Stole somethin' then shot my way clear when I was caught." He shrugged. "What the hell difference does it make?"

Burkhauser pushed him away. "Get on back there. I'll be all right."

Tanner hesitated. "Don't you go dyin' on me, you hear?"

"I'll live to see Texas," Burkhauser promised. "Now leave me the hell alone." He sagged against a heavy piece of furniture, resting his shoulder and head; he still kept his hand on his pistol.

Jim McClintock, acting as scout for the Army, didn't think it was possible to surprise Calaveras; the cavalry simply made too much noise and if a man's ears weren't full of wax, he could hear them two miles away, which would give Calaveras enough time to get his horses and make for the mountains.

The only hope McClintock had was that Calaveras would think it was Mexican cavalry and not pull out at all. But that was a slim hope.

You had to give Murdo credit; he sure was pushing his command, making an all-night march of it, and it was shortly before dawn that they came within sight of Spaniard's walled rancho. Murdo urged his horse forward and sided McClintock and they rode at the head of the double column, the wagons lumbering along, curb chains making a racket.

Ahead they could see brief flashes that marked gunfire but they were too far away to hear the shooting. Murdo turned to his ever-present bugler and made a mistake.

"Sound the charge," he said, thereby identifying the troops as United States Cavalry.

McClintock tried to knock the bugle away from the man's lips, but Murdo was between them and he failed; the rippling, clear tones of the horn broke over the column and the cavalry thundered ahead, leaving behind choking dust and the knowledge in McClintock's mind that they would be too late.

Murdo had his command to attend to and wheeled back to take charge of the wagons and artillery; they broke into a run, carriages bouncing and rattling and McClintock let them all pass on. He dropped back to the quartermaster wagons and sided a wrinkle-faced sergeant.

"Cavalry's always runnin' ain't they?" the sergeant asked. "And you know, when we get there, you'll find 'em waitin' for us."

"Where's the contract surgeon's wagon?"

The sergeant jerked his thumb over his shoulder. "Next wagon."

McClintock wheeled out, sided the ambulance and swung to the seat. The surgeon was a young man in a yellow oilskin duster; he looked at

223

McClintock and said, "You don't look like a man with a complaint."

"Go straight in," McClintock said tightly. "There'll be wounded men in the house."

"Ain't there always?" the surgeon said. "Won't hurt to hurry a little, I suppose." He slapped the reins against the backs of the team and got a quicker pace out of them. Another wagon, carrying supplies, tent, and orderlies, kept pace.

McClintock couldn't wait; he left the wagon, mounted his horse and rode on toward the rubble and breech in the wall. The *banditos* were gone, leaving only their dead, and from the number McClintock could gauge the ferocity of the fighting. He saw the smashed door and flung off and ran inside.

The artillerymen were dismounted in the yard; their sergeant was bawling them to order, and Major Murdo was inside, taking stock of the situation.

McClintock found Will Beech right away; he was limping from a bullet wound in the thigh and a bloody bandage circled his head. Beech said, "Over here, Jim," and took McClintock into the library.

The dead were stretched out in the hall and covered with blankets and when McClintock saw a pair of hand-tooled, expensive boots he bent and pulled the blanket back from Jacob Spaniard's face.

Then he stepped into the library with Beech; the badly wounded were there and he saw Burkhauser propped in a large leather chair. The old man opened his eyes when Jim knelt by him; he said, "Wanted to come out and greet you but—"

"Aw, shut your old fool mouth," McClintock said, his eyes filling up. He sniffed and wiped a finger across his nose. "We got a doc. You'll get fixed up all right. Hell, ain't you always gettin' shot?" He turned to Beech. "The wagons ought to be rollin' in. Fetch him."

Beech nodded and went out, moving as fast as he could. Finley Burkhauser watched him go then gripped McClintock's hand. "Go to your wife, boy. Damn it, she's lived in hell, worryin'."

"The doc'll be here—"

"I promise to wait for him," Burkhauser said. "Get out of here now."

McClintock hesitated, then left the library and went up the stairs two at a time. He hammered on May's door, then she stepped out of her mother's room, saw him and rushed into his arms, kissing him. He held her for a moment, then put her away.

"You're all right, May?"

"Yes." She looked at him steadily. "I heard the bugle and the horses leaving. Is it all over?"

"The *banditos* are gone," he said. "May, your father's dead."

"I want to see him."

"I don't think you—"

"Jim, please."

He sighed and took her downstairs; the Army was everywhere, in complete charge and the contract surgeon was setting up in the library. McClintock took her to the row of covered men and peeled the blanket back from Jacob Spaniard's face.

She looked at him for a full minute, then nodded and he put the blanket back. "I hope he wasn't full of regret and disappointment in that moment, you know, when he was hit. It seems that's all he saw in life, disappointment, regret. Nothing was ever right for him, or his way. It's a terrible way to be."

"Do you want to stay here, May? The ranch is yours and—"

"I'll go where you go," she said.

"You and your mother are rich now; all his gold is yours."

She looked at him carefully, then said, "Jim, if you're suggesting that I've made a mistake, don't do it. Don't ever suggest it or think it." She turned her head and looked around. "Where's Mr. Burkhauser?"

"In the library," he said. "He's bad hurt, May."

"Go to him. Please, I want you to." She touched him lightly. "I know what he means to you."

"'We'll both go," he said gently and put his arm around her.

226

TEN

At dawn the contract surgeon was finished; the library reeked of chloroform, sickeningly sweet. An Army detail had taken the dead outside and guard posts were established around the yard and house.

The *pistoleros* were not under arrest, yet they stood by the well, and they were watched closely. Major Murdo set up his command post in the huge hall and McClintock found him there, burdened by details.

"Major, are you arresting the *pistoleros*?"

"I haven't made up my mind what to do with them," Murdo admitted. "Frankly, they're civilians and the province of the Texas Rangers. I'll accept your recommendation, Jim."

"Let 'em go."

"Release them?" He looked intently at McClintock. "In six months you'll be tracking them down for one crime or another. It seems that—" He shrugged. "All right, I don't want to be saddled with them to the border." He scribbled an order on a piece of paper and handed it to McClintock. "Give this to the sergeant."

McClintock went out and found him by the well, a large, melon-bellied man who read the order without change of expression. Then the sergeant gave an order and the soldiers who had been loitering about fell in a formation and marched to the stable area.

Pete Tanner watched them go, then said, "What is it, Jim?"

"Take your horses and what you need and leave," McClintock said.

The *pistoleros* stood silent, listening, but Tanner showed surprise.

"You're turnin' us loose, Jim?"

"It's a dirty trick, ain't it? You're wanted on the Texas side of the river, and in Mexico you'll be fair game for any man who can stick a knife in you because they're afraid of you and hate you because you've made them afraid. But I can't help any of that, Pete. We're goin' to keep our bargain, so get your horses, help yourself to what provisions you want and scatter."

"You think any of us will ever make another start, Jim?"

"I don't know. Depends on how far you ride and what you do when you get there. Put away your pistols and take up a plow or a scoop shovel, somethin' as far away from trouble as you can get. Some of you may make it."

Tanner nodded. "The old bear goin' to make it all right?"

"I don't know. The doc got the bullet out, but he doesn't know either. So long, Pete. And good luck."

"You really mean that, don't you?" He laughed softly. "Jim, I just found out somethin': I just found out you never hated any of us. A man on the run, lookin' over his shoulder all the time, gets to figurin' that every man with a badge hates him. Hate's like a disease, Jim; a man catches it pretty quick and it lasts a long time. *Adios amigo*."

"*Via con Dios*," McClintock said.

He went back inside the house. Murdo had an officer and two sergeants taking inventory of the safe, and packing the coin and paper money in rifle cases. When McClintock came up Murdo said, "Well, he certainly was a rich man. I've talked to the wife; she wants to return to Texas and live. We'll escort her, of course, and handle all details." He let a worried frown build and consulted his watch. "What the hell can have happened to Lieutenant Bingham at the pass?" He shrugged and put his watch away. "Before I forget it, the surgeon wants to see you."

McClintock found him stretched out on the floor in the hall near the library door; he was not asleep although he seemed to be. He sat up when McClintock hunkered down. "I might as well tell you straight out; there's not much hope for him."

"How long?"

The surgeon's shoulders rose and fell slightly. "Who knows? He's old but he's got the constitution of a bull. Five hours maybe. A little more; who can say?" He wiped a hand over his face as though trying to wash away the weariness. "He's out of the chloroform. He wants to see you."

McClintock nodded and went in; some cots had been set up and Finley Burkhauser's was in a corner. He rolled his eyes slightly to watch Jim McClintock approach.

"Want to Indian wrestle?" Burkhauser asked.

"I can't stand bein' beat," McClintock admitted. "How're you makin' it?"

"Guess I won't this time, old horse. Would you do a man a favor, Jim?"

"Sure, you just name it."

"I want to die in Texas, Jim. Get me back." He reached out and gripped McClintock's arm with surprising strength. "You can do it, boy. Use a travois. I'll last. No complaints. Hell, they're as easy ridin' as a hammock on a shady porch. Jim, do it."

"I'll see what the doc says."

"The doc, hell, it's me that's askin'. I want a promise."

"All right," McClintock said. "I'll get ready to leave."

He told Major Murdo about it and got no strong objection; Murdo figured it was Ranger business and he had his own hands full with no word from Bingham and Mrs. Spaniard to safely escort back across the river, and wounded men to carry back; he had a hundred pressing details to handle and he did not need one more.

McClintock found May and drew her to one side; he didn't waste words with her. "Finley's dyin', May. He wants to do it in Texas. Will you come with me?"

"Wherever you go, Jim."

"Your mother—"

"She'll be taken care of. It was never the world I wanted to protect her from, Jim. I'll throw some things together." She patted him on the arm and went upstairs while he went out and across to the stable yard.

He still had Calaveras's horse; he selected another, one owned by a *pistolero* who would never need it again. Two enlisted men helped him build the travois and cover it. Another went to the house and put together a snack of provisions and brought four canteens full of water.

"You figurin' to cross the desert alone?" one of the men asked. "There's some talk goin' around that Calaveras and his bunch didn't try to get through the pass. If they're out there on the desert—"

"I don't figure he is," McClintock said. He looked to the mountains. "That's his home, and a man heads there when trouble gets bad."

"Then how come he didn't try to get through

the pass?" the soldier asked. "He's got to be somewhere."

"You worry about it enough and they may make you a corporal," McClintock told him and led the horses across the yard. May came out with a bundle of clothes and blankets wrapped in a ground cloth and the surgeon had Burkhauser brought out on a litter. While he was being fastened on the travois, the surgeon took McClintock to one side and gave him a small leather case.

"I've got him pretty well loaded against pain. Sometime tonight it will wear off. Stick this in his arm and press the plunger."

McClintock nodded and put the case in his coat pocket. "The travois is pretty easy ridin', but if he starts bleedin'—"

"He's bled so much now I doubt there's enough in him to leak out," the surgeon said. "I'll never figure out what keeps some of these men going." He offered his hand briefly, then turned and went back into the house.

Will Beech came out. He was bearded, thinner, more grave now; he wore a pair of pistols very casually for he knew how to use them now and a man could tell that just by looking at him.

"Jim, if I was to quit the railroad, would you recommend me to the captain when I signed up?"

"Any time," McClintock said. "Come with us, Will."

He shook his head. "The major's talking about taking a company into the mountains in pursuit of Calaveras. I volunteered as a scout." He grinned. "Now that's what I call getting big for the breeches."

"If you ain't careful, you'll be gettin' a reputation."

"Well, I sure as hell don't want to go back to hunting down lost keepsakes and throwing drunks off trains," Beech said. "I don't want to go back to the railroad and live off my memories, Jim. I can do things, you know." He took a deep breath and slapped his rib cage. "Jim, there's an awful lot of Texas and a man just can't afford to miss any of it, can he?"

"You're all right, Will," McClintock said and helped May on her horse. He mounted and turned out of the yard, dragging the travois, and he never looked back at the place once he left it. Before him stretched the rolling desert, tawny and shimmering under the climbing sun.

May rode by his side for a time, then she looked at him and he reached out and lifted her from her horse to his and rode with his arms around her.

"It's a long way home," she said softly. "Is going home always so sad, Jim?" She put her head against his shoulder and rested that way. "For years now I've thought about being free. Now I am. I can have the life I want and I wonder where to start."

"Well, I've saved some money. We can start by buyin' a house and you can cook supper for me every night."

The wound in Will Beech's leg was throbbing when he reported to Major Murdo, but he managed to limp very little and certainly didn't waste time when Murdo motioned for him to sit on one of the camp stools.

"I've heard no word from Lieutenant Bingham at the pass," Murdo said. "I've asked Lieutenant Rice to report here. Since you've agreed to scout, our best move is to send a company up there and look the situation over."

Rice came up, a man in his early thirties; he saluted, then sat down. He glanced at Will Beech, at the bandage around his thigh, and the other around his head, and he glanced at the pair of .44 pistols Beech wore, then he said, "You're one of the Texas Rangers, aren't you?"

It was in Beech to correct this; he was that honest, but the words wouldn't come out. He looked at Murdo then understood that the major also took it for granted that he was a Ranger and the pleasure of it filled Beech with a new strength and the pain he felt seemed to go away and he merely nodded.

"Mr. Beech has already been into the mountains and Calaveras's camp," Murdo said and the lieutenant's eyes widened and a new, profound respect came into his manner. "He'll guide your company, Mr. Rice. I would suggest that you concur with his opinions, and follow his advice even though it might conflict with your military judgment."

"I quite understand," Rice said and smiled. "I'll give Mr. Beech no trouble."

Beech was so flattered that he made a modest motion with his hand and Murdo said, "Mr. Rice, the last thing I want to happen is to have rapid-fire weapons fall into this bandit's hands, and I fear—since I've heard nothing from the detail—that this possibility has become an actuality. It is very important that you relieve the detail, and return here to base with the weapons. If you have to chase over half of Mexico to do it, then that's what you'll do. Are your orders clear, Mr. Rice?"

"Crystal, sir."

"Major," Beech said, "I would suggest that Mr. Rice's company shed a little military equipment before we leave."

"How do you mean that?" Murdo asked.

"Well, Major, with all the trappings the cavalry carries around, you can hear them a country mile. And Calaveras has big ears." He paused, trying to remember the things he had learned from McClintock. "I'd suggest carbines and sidearms, canteens, and blankets. Dry rations for men and mounts."

"Surely saddles—" Rice began, then stopped when Beech shook his head.

"I want every man as light as he can be," Beech said. "Not only to save the horses, but to give us staying power and speed if we have to run Calaveras down."

"Unorthodox," Murdo said, "but MacKenzie did it against the Comanches. Very well, Mr. Rice. Have your men ready to ride in forty minutes."

"I can make that a half hour, sir."

"So much the better," Murdo said. Rice left and Beech got up and favored his bad leg. "You're sure that won't—"

"Just a nick," Beech lied and hobbled away, thinking that all these men were brave men and if he could only pretend long enough, fool them long enough, they might think that he was like them. He went over to the stable area and had the sergeant there pick out a good horse for him and while the animal was being cut out, Beech supposed that all his life he would be seeking the company of brave men, studying them, trying to learn from them, and all the time hoping that some of it would rub off on himself.

When the company left, Beech rode with Lieutenant Rice and it was good to ride at the head of the double column; he knew he wouldn't forget this feeling of genuine importance. Rice, riding alongside with his campaign hat tipped forward over the bridge of his nose, said, "The head of the pass, Mr. Beech?"

Instead of speaking, Beech muffled the inclination and made a straight out cutting motion with his hand—silent talk, McClintock called it—and in that way indicated the pass as their destination.

There was no sign of the *banditos* and Beech kept looking left and right and scanning the high ground ahead of them. Then they started up, single file, spread out; that was his order because he didn't want them bunched up if Calaveras had the Gatling guns.

The day was a smoulder of heat and merciless sun and they kept climbing, working their way up toward the summit. Beech motioned for Rice and the others to follow and he went on ahead for fifty yards, a bit of foolishness, he supposed, but he felt that it was his duty to draw the first fire. His head throbbed from his scalp wound and sweat stung it constantly and the dust settled on his face and ate him raw, especially around the collar and his leg was simply the fits, but he kept his face as inscrutable as an Indian's.

A pistol shot ahead and the bullet whanging off a nearby rock caused him to fling off; he drew his gun and bellied down and began to eel forward like McClintock would have done. Rice and the company was under cover and he waved for them to remain down and went on alone.

Ten minutes of dragging himself along brought him to the lip of a small pocket; it was littered with dead soldiers. Only Bingham was alive, barely. He had been blinded and there was a horrible wound in his stomach, with the flies bothering the spread of blood and torn flesh.

Beech almost threw up, but he choked it down and said, "Bingham, hang on, man. Rice is here with a whole company." Then he stood up and signaled and Rice came forward with the command and when he dropped down into the pocket, Beech had already bathed Bingham's face and put a bandage over his eyes.

"Heard—your horses," Bingham said.

"It's all right, man," Rice said, a catch in his voice. One of the Gatling guns and ammunition carriage remained and Rice motioned for the sergeant to go over and have a look at it. Then he climbed the perimeter with Beech and dead Mexicans lay in a scatter about and it was the story of how Bingham and his handful had held out.

The sergeant climbed up and saluted. "You can see the tracks where one of the guns and carriage was taken away, sir."

"Thank you, Sergeant." He looked at Beech. "Mr. Bingham and his command fought to the last man to hang onto the other one. We'll make good use of it if we can find Calaveras's camp, Beech."

"I can find it," Beech said.

"How do you suppose they got up here without Bingham hearing them?" Rice asked.

"On their bellies. Bingham never got a chance to hold them off with the Gatling guns."

The sergeant came back. "Sir, Mr. Bingham just died. Shall I form a burial detail?"

Rice nodded and took off his hat and mopped his sweating face. "If you have no objections, Beech."

"No, there's no objection," Beech said softly and watched Rice walk away. They faced death very calmly, he thought.

Burial was a matter of piling rocks on the bodies and leaving markers; it did not take more than forty minutes and Lieutenant Rice made his service brief, then gave the order to mount up.

The Gatling gun was mounted on a two-wheeled carriage, the tongue serving as trails when dropped. The ammunition carriage was similar and they were hooked together with a clevis and pulled by two horses. Calaveras, in departing, split ammunition and gun into two units so that a single horseman could pull them and in doing so left a trail that Beech had no difficulty in following.

Even without the trail to follow, Beech figured that Calaveras was heading for his nest; a man always seemed to run for home when trouble got thick, and Calaveras had plenty of it. He had lost too many men trying to take Spaniard's *hacienda*, and judging by the dead men at the head of the pass, Second Lieutenant Charles Butler Bingham had made him pay so dearly for that one Gatling gun that Calaveras had lost his taste for the other.

Moving along, Beech was surprised to find that he could keep his bearing, his sense of direction. He had learned from McClintock how to travel near the top of the ridge, but down from it so that at no time did he stand out against the bright sky.

He kept the command in the rocks, kept them moving, often dismounted and leading the horses, and finally, when the going got too rough, he had the Gatling gun dismounted from the carriage and packed, wheels on one horse, tongue and axel on another, and gun on another. It forced troopers to walk, but he made no apology for that.

That evening he found a high place for them and they made cold camp and there was no talking allowed. Beech and Albert Rice sat together, washing down dried meat and biscuits with swigs from their canteens. Rice spoke in a whisper. "I haven't seen one sign of life all day." He looked at Will Beech. "How do you figure that?"

Beech needed wisdom, so he chewed slowly and drank slowly and thought it over carefully and this meditation gave weight to his words. "My guess is that Calaveras is licking his wounds. He got stung badly, you know. Cut down to half strength at least. No commander can take a pasting like that and not feel it." He ate some more, drank some more and Rice waited for the prophet to drop his next pearl of wisdom. "I'd say that Calaveras was back at his camp, trying to pull together an effective fighting force. He didn't get the gold, and there'll be grumbling about that. Your Army gets paid, Lieutenant, but Calaveras's lives off the loot. No loot, no pay."

"We've got to get that Gatling gun back," Rice said.

"Sure, sure, we'll get it back." He was surprised at his own confidence for he didn't feel confident at all. He corked his canteen and stretched out on the earth.

Rice said, "Will, I want you to know that every man in the company feels better because you're along on this."

"Better get some sleep," Beech said, almost gruffly. But he turned on his side and put his cheek in his palm and prayed that the flaws in his character wouldn't show. It filled him with a sense of haste, to get this mission over before he revealed himself to these men. He didn't think he would be able to stand it if they knew.

Nothing woke him; he was just awake and the air was so cold a man could see his breath. He got Rice up and the sergeants stirred and then the company was up and moving about as silently as possible. The second lieutenants in charge of the squads made their way to Rice's position and awaited orders.

They all kept looking at Will Beech and finally Rice said, "How much farther do you think, Will?"

Beech was rummaging for rations; he looked up and peered at them in the predawn darkness. "No more than two miles." He pointed to the southwest where a ridge ran ragged and stony. "Follow that. We'll go afoot now. Have the Gatling gun mounted and wrap the wheels in blankets. We'll hand pull it. Carry it when we have to."

Albert Rice looked at the others, then spoke in an awed voice. "You mean to say we camped the night within—?"

"Better to hit them before dawn," Beech said. "Mexicans like their women and wine and they'd been away a spell and every one of them will have some catching up to do. They'll be rolled in with a woman and smelling like sour grapes."

Rice had a point to make. "Will, an accidental shot, one mistake by any of the troopers and Calaveras would have heard it."

"Yes," Beech said. "But I didn't expect you to make any. Better have some rations. Want to be moving in fifteen minutes."

One of the second lieutenants, a pale-cheeked, Academy fresh officer, said, "By God, that's nerve all right."

"You heard Mr. Beech's orders," Rice said. "See that they're carried out."

The three young officers saluted and left and Rice hunkered down. "Will, we can't charge Calaveras's camp with one company, dismounted."

"I know." He took a cartridge from his belt and made some marks in the earth. "This is the ridge we're on. It makes a long sweep around, in a southerly direction." He made another cross mark. "Move down off the flanks and you come to a timbered valley. Follow it and you run into what appears to be a rock wall. There's a fissure in it maybe eight foot wide. This is heavily guarded because it's the entrance to meadow and water, and Calaveras's camp." He looked at Rice to make sure he understood. "In plain English, it's a pocket with one way out." He put an X on the perimeter of the kidney-shaped line he had drawn. "There's a foot trail there, but we could seal it with some powder. I'd say three pounds would bring down that whole wall in one hell of a slide. It might drive Calaveras out through the pass. You could have the Gatling gun and most of the command set up there, waiting. I don't think he could get through."

"We don't have any powder," Rice said. "Of course, we could empty carbine cartridges. We're using the full seventy grain infantry charge."

"Won't be necessary," Beech said and picked

up two gallon canteens. "I filled these before we left the *hacienda*." He grinned. "That artillery captain is one nice fella. Fuses and everything. Got four men who can plant this?"

"I'll get them for you," Rice said and walked away.

Beech sat on the ground and nibbled at his rations. The pain in his leg was nowhere as severe as it had been, although walking on it had been pure hell. Yet he supposed that it had helped the wound; he'd heard of things like that, that it was good not to baby yourself when you were hurt. The quicker a man got up and moved around, the better off he was.

Rice came back with three men. "Corporal Allen was in the engineers; he's handled powder. These two men have been miners."

Beech explained that he wanted charges set so that the whole back wall of the canyon came rumbling down and Allen listened, then said, "Take four good charges, Mr. Beech. You've got two gallons of powder? I can split that up. Placed right it'll slide the whole rim to the meadow."

"The job is yours," Beech said and gave him the canteens. He glanced at Rice. "We should be able to make it to the head of the pass and set up positions by dawn." He glanced at the sky. "I'd say it's two hours off. Allen, that should be plenty of time for you."

"Sure, plenty, Mr. Beech."

"Then get going. Touch it off just before sunrise and get the hell out of there. Don't try to join us. Hole up in this area and wait for us."

Allen nodded; Rice dismissed them with a glance and a few minutes later the three men left the camp. Rice and the rest of the company was ready to move out, and Beech led them down the steep flank of the mountain, picking a way that was not too dangerous for the men who had to carry the Gatling gun and ammunition. The carriage had been left behind and ammunition split up so that each man carried some of it.

Beech used the game trails, working down, and finally reaching the timber. They could move faster now and within an hour they seemed to come to the end of it; a sheer rock wall faced them at a distance of sixty yards.

With motions he dispersed the command; there was no talking at all. The Gatling gun and ammunition was positioned so that it covered the entrance, and the troopers were scattered to the flank so they could rake anyone making it through with a broadside fire. Deadfalls were brought up to make a bunker around the Gatling gun and crew and there was nothing to do but wait while the sky grew imperceptibly lighter.

The waiting was hell for Beech and he reasoned that he had brought them this far on bluff. Now that was ended. Bullets were going to fly and what a man was was going to show.

A dull boom interrupted his thoughts; it sounded like distant thunder followed by four evenly spaced echoes, then there was the trembling rumble of earth sliding and Calaveras's camp came suddenly awake.

In the light of the new day dust rose in a high thick cloud and for fifteen minutes there was nothing, no movement save the stirring of dust; it was beginning to settle now, filtering down through the timber that hid them, layering their clothes and settling on carbine and pistol barrels.

Beech waited, a pair of .44 self-cockers in his hands. Rice was in the bunker with the gun crew, then there was the sound of horses running and they burst from the pass in pairs; Rice gave the command to fire and the Gatling gun cut them down like some invisible mower. Horses and men fell thrashing to either side and in front of the entrance and the troopers held their fire for this wasn't the big push; this was just the first frightened ones trying to get out.

No more came through, then Rice signaled Beech, who bellied over. "They're setting up a barricade across the pass," Rice said. He had hardly finished speaking when the captured Gatling gun began to chatter and bullets pumped into the logs, showering them with splinters.

One of the soldiers jumped to the Gatling, meaning to return the burst, but a bullet broke his shoulder, spun him around and flung him down.

Rice's eyes were wide and he said, "We've got to get the Goddamned gun," and even as he said it he knew no one was going to leap the barricade and charge it.

He took Beech by the arm. "Where's Calaveras, damn it? Why doesn't he charge?"

"My guess is he's working his way up the slide to the rim," Beech said. "If he can get most of his men up there, he'll circle and hit you from the rear and drive you right into the Gatling gun."

The Mexicans were holding fire, waiting, and Rice and his command waited too. Rice crouched against the deadfalls and sweat stood out on his forehead in small beads. Then one would swell heavy and roll down his cheeks.

Beech checked his pistols; he couldn't remember if he had fired or not. He hadn't so he snapped them closed and looked around. "Any of you feel lucky?" he asked, then suddenly hoisted himself over the deadfall and flopped to the ground.

The Mexicans were taken by surprise and before they could swing their gun, Rice began to fire; one of the sergeants was cranking the handle while another fed slides of ammunition into it. The sergeant pumped out a hundred and fifty rounds and kept the Mexicans down while Beech made his dash for a clutter of rocks near the pass. At any moment he expected to be cut down, but the bullet with his name on it never touched him. He fell gasping into the rocks, still clutching his unfired revolvers, then he jerked in surprise as the pink-faced lieutenant and a sergeant flopped down near him.

"Couldn't let you go it alone," the lieutenant said and grinned although his eyes were round with fright. The sergeant made a grim face and wiped his mouth with the back of his hand.

Beech rested against the rocks to still his trembling; his leg was a flame of pain now and it was bleeding again. Without taking his eyes off the pass, a distance of fifteen yards, he said, "They didn't shoot much, did they?" When neither answered him, he looked around, looked at them and looked back. Three troopers lay sprawled in the open and the ground had been cut by bullets; they pocked the dirt along the route he had taken and he realized then that he had been so frightened he hadn't realized he had survived this hail.

The sergeant laughed and worked his jaws on his tobacco. He carried a pair of long-barreled Colts pistols, as did the lieutenant. "What's next, Mr. Beech. I'm goin' to stick damned close to you from here on in."

Beech studied the pass. The Mexicans couldn't really see them crouched in the rocks, nor could they swivel the gun without exposing themselves. Their best chance, he figured, was to rush them, fight it out hand-to-hand, and hope their luck held.

"Let's go," Beech said and hobbled to his feet, running, limping, driving himself that short, yet remote distance. He could hear the lieutenant and the sergeant, then suddenly he was there, jumping over the barrel of the gun and having a rifle go off in his face. How the bullet missed him he would never know; he fired pointblank, killed the Mexican, then somehow the lieutenant and the sergeant got into it and they fired and cocked and fired. It was all powder smoke and bullets and sound. Rice charged with the rest of the company and men seemed to be lying all around Beech and he kept shooting until his pistols were empty, then he fell on the ground and remained there for there was no time to reload.

When the firing stopped he couldn't believe it, so he sat up and discovered that he was not wounded. There were several bullet holes in his shirt sleeve, and one had gone through his hat, exiting with a ragged tear.

The young lieutenant was standing with one of his pistols holstered, the other tucked under his arm, and he was clamping both hands to a wound just above the knee.

The sergeant was chewing his tobacco, unhurt, and not yet accustomed to the miracle. Rice took possession of the Gatling gun and the ammunition carriage; he ordered the dead bandits pushed out of the way and the barricade struck.

Beech reloaded his pistols and holstered them

and when he came up, Rice turned and looked at him for a long, silent moment. "Do we pursue, Mr. Beech?"

"Get back to the horses," Beech said, feeling that the sooner they were out of there the better.

Rice nodded, mistaking Beech's meaning. "Right. We can't let Calaveras find the horses." He left then, shouting orders and within minutes the wounded were littered and they were pulling out, going back through the timber and working higher to make the ridge where the horseholders waited.

One man went on ahead, a hardy trooper who climbed like a goat and before they were half-way there, the horseholders were starting down. They paused because they needed rest and time to reorganize. Rice gave them ten minutes, then came over and sat down near Will Beech. "Cigar?" he said, offering one.

Beech didn't care for one, but he accepted it, not wishing to offend Rice. He took a light from the lieutenant, then Rice said, "Will, a man doesn't know what to say at a time like this."

"About what?" Beech asked, genuinely puzzled.

"The Mexicans shot a tube of ammunition at you when you made that dash. I wouldn't have given a nickel for your chances."

"I didn't know it," Beech admitted. "I was too scared."

Rice looked at him like a man will when he is

being joked with and didn't want to be. Then he said, "All right, Will, have it your way, but I'm writing this up to send to your commanding officer."

What commanding officer? Beech thought and knew a moment of panic. "Why don't you just forget it?" he suggested. "If we don't get off our ass, we'll never overtake Calaveras."

Albert Rice laughed and slapped Beech on the shoulder. "You're the damnedest fella I ever met, Will. You sure are. Don't you ever run out of steam?"

McClintock stopped often to see how Burkhauser was holding up. Life in the old man was a shallow flame detectable in the pupils of his eyes. His complexion was gray like putty, but he lived; he could manage a smile but he did not speak, as though he were using all his strength to live and did not dare waste any on words.

In the afternoon it turned off cloudy and a rainstorm built over the mountains behind them and then just before sunset the sun came through the lead-colored sky. The mountains were all gray, dark, with clouds covering the peaks like heavy frosting on a dark cake.

McClintock gathered brush and built a small fire and cooked a meal, making some soup in a pot and Burkhauser ate it, a spoonful at a time. May fixed coffee and fried some meat and left-over potatoes. Burkhauser closed his eyes and seemed to sleep and they sat away from him and talked softly.

The break in the clouds closed and the sun vanished and night was not far away. McClintock kept looking at the desert, letting his eyes sweep clear around the horizon, then he concentrated on a far-out place, watching a raise of dust.

"Mexican cavalry," he said, pointing. "They're in formation. *Banditos* wouldn't ride that way." He reached for the coffeepot and filled his cup again. "No use runnin'. They saw the fire."

The Mexican cavalry came on, a troop, led by a young lieutenant in a bright uniform and wearing a waxed mustache. They stopped a short way from the fire, then the lieutenant rode in alone and sat his horse, looking down at them. "Ah, we meet again, señor. You do not remember me?"

"I remember you," McClintock said. "Rivas was the name and you took gold from Jacob Spaniard."

"*Sí*, I take gold from many people." He looked intently at May. "Many times I have seen you in a carriage, señorita. Permit me to ask what you are doing out here with this man?"

"My father is sending them both back to Texas," she said coolly. "If there is anything else you wish to know, you will have to ask him."

The lieutenant bowed. "All goes well at the *rancho*?"

"The Army is there," May said. "Would you like to talk to the commander?"

Lieutenant Rivas laughed and shook his head. "I regret to say that our duties carry us in another direction. The pleasure will have to await another time."

"I don't suppose you've seen any *banditos*?" McClintock asked.

"Oh, now, señor. I have searched for them everywhere but they are ghosts. When they are one place, I am always in another." He shrugged and smiled. "But someday we will meet. It is a matter of time and patience." He touched his fingers to his hat and backed his horse. "*Adios*, señors, señorita."

"You be sure and stay out of trouble," McClintock urged.

Rivas laughed. "I will live far longer than you, señor."

He rejoined his patrol and they turned away, riding in an easterly direction. McClintock sighed and got up and removed his hand from beneath his coat; the palm was sweaty from gripping the smooth butt of his pistol. Finley Burkhauser's arm slipped over the side of the travois and his .44 fell to the ground, still cocked.

McClintock walked over, picked it up, let the hammer down, then handed it back to him. "I thought you was asleep."

"I had a bead right on his wishbone," Burkhauser said. "Ain't we spent enough time here, boy?"

"Yeah," McClintock said and kicked out the fire.

May gathered the skillet and pot, then mounted her own horse and they left that place and moved north toward the river yet a half a day ahead of them. Night came like the slow closing of a blind in the sky and when it was fully dark, the clouds started to drift apart, letting through strong moonlight.

McClintock knew it would be best to stop and give Burkhauser some relief from the bobbing cradle motion of the travois, but he knew what the old man wanted and kept the horses at a walk, pacing out the night without more than five-minute stops between their supper camp and the Rio Grande.

The Mexican village was graveyard silent when they passed through to the ferry. McClintock had to wake the man to take them across and the Rangers from the station on the other side saw the lantern on the ferry and two of them came down to the landing to see who was traveling at that time of the night.

McClintock knew both of them; he said nothing, just jerked his thumb toward the travois and they went back and gently eased Burkhauser to the ground. His face was grim with pain, and washed of all color. Yet the light was still in his eyes and he looked for Jim McClintock, who knelt down and took his hand.

Digging his fingers into the dirt, Burkhauser brought some to his nose and sniffed, then he sighed. "That's Texas." His voice was very weak, almost a whisper. "Been smellin' Texas all my life. No man could fool me." He saw the two Rangers there. "That you, Adams, Petersen?" He gripped McClintock's hand, then the strength slowly left his fingers and the hand fell away.

McClintock turned away, choking back a sob, then it came out of him and May went to him and put her arms around him. The two Rangers stood there a minute, then Adams said, "By God, he was just some punkins, that's all I got to say. A whole team and a dog under the wagon, that's what he was!"

McClintock wiped his eyes and blew his nose. Petersen said, "Jim, if it's all right, we'll take him on in a wagon."

McClintock nodded, not looking at them; he walked to the edge of the river with May and sat down, his arm around her. "There's a little bit of a man that dies every day, ain't there? Right now I'm thinkin' just what the hell it's goin' to be like without him." He looked at her. "Help me, May. Please."

"Yes, Jim." She got up and took his hand, making him get up too. "We're in Texas, Jim. He wanted us to be here too. Remember that. We're where we belong now."

He nodded and they turned to their horses, leading them, walking slowly, their arms around each other, toward the town a half mile away.

Captain George Fuller fell the entire company out for the funeral and the governor wired his personal message of regret and it seemed to Jim McClintock that half the town of Laredo was there at the cemetery.

Afterward, he was summoned to Fuller's office, nodded into a chair, offered a glass of whiskey and a cigar. Finally Fuller said, "Jim, we've lost more than a man. We've lost a tradition."

"Yeah, I know. But he wouldn't see it that way. Captain, I'm goin' to be as good as he was. His boots will fit me. Damn it, sir, I can grow."

"He liked you best of all," Fuller said. "He told me that fifty times if he told me once." He wiped a hand across his mouth and drew deeply on his cigar. "Jim, I'm going to write out your orders this afternoon. I think a change will be good for you. New faces, new responsibilities. What do you say?"

"I'll go where you send me, Captain. Ain't I always?"

"I expected you to say that. For some years now I've been offering Burkhauser a promotion and he's always turned it down; he was a captain in the Army, you know, a man with the experience and ability to command. But he never wanted a desk job. So I'm going to jump you on the promotion list, Jim. I understand they're having a little fence cutting trouble around Palestine, so I've been ordered to recommend a man to head a detachment. I'm going to send you, Lieutenant McClintock. I expect you can leave on the eastbound tomorrow night."

"Yes, sir, I can do that."

"Good. And I'd like to meet your wife before you leave." He smiled. "Perhaps we could have dinner tonight at the hotel."

"That's fine," McClintock said. "Will that be all, Captain?" He got up when Fuller nodded, then turned to the door, stopping there. "Lieutenant? I'll be damned!"

"You'll cuss me for it, just as I cursed the man who chained me to a desk."

"I'll try to remember that and keep it under my breath," McClintock said and went out. He untied his horse after shouldering his way through a ring of Rangers.

One grinned and said, "Is it a fact, Jim, that this here animal is the personal property of that famous bandit, Calaveras?"

"Higgins, for once you've got the story straight," McClintock said, flipping up.

"I'll give you a hundred dollars for him," another said. "Cash."

"Not five hundred," McClintock told him.

"Maybe you'd just let me ride him a bit then," Higgins suggested.

McClintock laughed and shook his head and rode out of the post, taking the road to town. He put the horse up in the stable and walked to the hotel; the clerk gave him the key and he went upstairs and found the room near the end of the hall. He knocked and May opened the door. She wore a cotton dress and she had washed her hair and braided it.

"Now ain't that a pretty sight," he said and kissed her. He stepped in and closed the door with his foot. A large wooden tub sat in the middle of the floor on spread newspapers. "Is that bath water I see there?"

"No, I made a tub of soup." She tried to hold her face straight, then burst out laughing. "What did the captain say besides hello and goodbye?"

"He was in a good humor," McClintock said and began to undress. "You want me to close my eyes?"

"Don't be funny. Just tell me what he said."

McClintock flung his clothes over the back of a chair and settled in the tub, sighing deeply. "Well, he's sending me to Palestine. Goin' to set up a detachment there." He looked at her and winked. "I'm in charge."

She clapped her hands together. "You got promoted to sergeant!"

"Lieutenant," he said and soaped himself. "I knew it was bound to happen; you just can't ignore true genius forever." He let a grin build. "On that kind of pay we can afford to raise kids. You feel like gettin' started on it?"

Color climbed steadily and deeply into her cheeks. "Why don't you bring the subject up again tonight?"

"Doggone, I believe I will." He handed her the washcloth. "You mind scrubbing my back?" He sat there and rocked slightly as she scrubbed him. "We'll have to leave on the eastbound tomorrow night."

"I rather expected that," she said.

"The captain's goin' to have dinner with us tonight in the hotel dinin' room. I'm glad you got a new dress."

"My only dress," she said. Then she slapped the wet washrag down on his head. "But since you're a lieutenant, I think I'll buy another one. Maybe two, if I find something I like."

He reached for her and he would have pulled her into the tub with him, clothes and all, but she yelped and darted out of his way. She shook her finger at him. "Behave yourself, Jim."

"Will you explain the rules to me?"

"Sometime, but it's better if you pick them up as you go along."

They went to the dining room at seven and sat down; the waiter served them coffee while they waited for George Fuller, then a boy came in with a note saying that he would be a bit late and to start without him.

After waiting another ten minutes, they ordered and took their time about eating, but McClintock was starting on his peach pie and Fuller hadn't yet appeared.

McClintock kept watching the arch leading to the hotel lobby and because of this he saw Will Beech as soon as he came in. Dust layered his clothes and he walked stiffly, as a man will after making a fast, uninterrupted ride of seventy miles. Beech searched them out and came directly to the table; McClintock signaled the waiter to bring another order and Beech sagged in the chair, letting his slight body go loose.

"You look like a man who's been hurryin' along," McClintock said. "The Army come back with you?"

"Way behind," Beech said. "Jim, the Army got the hell licked out of them. Calaveras led the cavalry on a merry chase while fifteen or twenty picked men climbed on foot to the top of the pass and captured one of the Gatling guns. The cavalry was away from the house, snipe hunting, when Calaveras attacked. He was after the gold, of course. Anyway Murdo drove him back; it was touch and go there for an hour or two. Murdo's force suffered fifteen percent casualties and Calaveras's even worse, but he had more men to start with." The waiter interrupted when he brought Beech his plate. "The upshot of it was that the damned Mexican cavalry had been waiting out there, watching us get shot up, then when Calaveras was just about ready to back off they swooped in and cleaned up." He stared at his plate a moment, then laughed. "I'll bet the lieutenant gets promoted to captain for this, and all these years he's been taking Calaveras's money to look the other way and give him a clear pass to the border."

McClintock said, "May's mother—"

"She's all right," Beech said. "She's riding in one of the quartermaster wagons, with the gold. You missed a good fight, Jim."

McClintock shook his head. "Will, I may have missed a fight, but take my word; none of 'em are any good. At least the Mexican government won't be raisin' hell about Murdo's punitive force. Don't you see? The Mexican government will be happy because it was their troops who licked the *banditos*. They got a chance to save face now and this whole thing will be talked over politely in Washington over whiskey and cigars." He sighed and refreshed his cup of coffee. "And the funny part of it is that none of them will know a damned thing about it, how it started, or anything. And it don't matter a bit whether they know or not." He sat there and stared for a moment at his coffee cup. "One time Finley

Burkhauser and I were camped on the Red in a grove of cottonwoods. There was a bird perched on one of the limbs, just sittin' there, rockin' very slightly. It was one of those warm Texas summer nights and the air was full of fireflies and then that bird just keeled over and fell to the ground and fluttered a little and died. It kind of got you, seein' that bird die like that. Finley started talkin' about how that bird's dyin' would affect the whole world and it made quite a story, how one thing would lead to another, movin' the hand of destiny this way and that until finally kings fell and fortunes were won and lost and armies met and fought and it all went back to that little bird that died there by the Red." He laughed under his breath. "It kind of makes some sense, don't it? I mean, you go far enough back in Jake Spaniard's life and a little bird kind of falls and starts it all."

"Jim, you're a philosopher," Beech said.

"Well, maybe, but fortunes were won and lost and armies met—"

"I wouldn't argue the theory," Beech admitted. "Sorry about Burkhauser. I just came from Fuller's office and he told me."

"He died with a bit of Texas in his hand," McClintock said. "He was a Texan from cradle to grave." He looked up and smiled and changed the subject. "I've been kicked up to a new assignment."

"Fuller told me."

"He got kind of gabby, didn't he?"

"I put in my application. He wants you to sign it before you leave," Beech said. "As soon as I finish recruit training, I want to join you in Palestine."

McClintock thought about it, then said, "Why then I guess I'm just goin' to have to hold a place open for you, Will."

"Thanks, Jim, I'll do my best."

"In three months you'll be askin' for a transfer," McClintock said. "I'll tell you one thing, commanding a detachment is no joke. A lot of responsibility there. Hair-brained ideas are out, you understand? Go by the book. Everything procedure."

"Yes, sir!" Beech smiled and left the room. Despite his wounds and fatigue he had a spring in his step. "And, Jim, thanks for everything."

"Well, May, it looks as if I have a new partner and a good one at that. I think Finley would approve."

Books are
produced in the
United States
using U.S.-based
materials

Books are printed
using a revolutionary
new process called
THINKtech™ that
lowers energy usage
by 70% and increases
overall quality

Books are
durable and
flexible
because of
smythe-sewing

Paper is
sourced using
environmentally
responsible
foresting methods
and the
paper is acid-free

Center Point Large Print
600 Brooks Road / PO Box 1
Thorndike, ME 04986-0001 USA

(207) 568-3717

US & Canada:
1 800 929-9108
www.centerpointlargeprint.com